PARANORMAL COZY MYSTERY

Schemes & Bad Dreams

TRIXIE SILVERTALE

Sittin' On A Goldmine
Productions L.L.C.

Sittin' On A Goldmine Productions, L.L.C.

info@sittinonagoldmine.co

www.sittinonagoldmine.co

ISBN: 978-1-952739-05-7

Cover Design © Sittin' On A Goldmine Productions, L.L.C.

Trixie Silvertale
Schemes and Bad Dreams: Paranormal Cozy Mystery : a novel / by Trixie Silvertale — 1st ed.

[1. Paranormal Cozy Mystery — Fiction. 2. Cozy Mystery — Fiction. 3. Amateur Sleuths — Fiction. 4. Female Sleuth — Fiction. 5. Wit and Humor — Fiction.] 1. Title.

This book contains some topics that may be trigger-ing, such as suicide. If you or someone you know is in need of assistance, please call the **National Suicide Prevention Lifeline**: 800-273-8255 (24/7)

International readers please consult this website and look for your country's listing: http://www.suicide.org/international-suicide-hotlines.html

CHAPTER 1

THE SKY SEEMS TOO BLUE. The wind, too crisp. The late summer sun, too golden. Despite the picturesque tableau that greets me as I roll out of my antique four-poster bed after a glorious snooze-in, my psychic senses are atingle with dread.

I may be half asleep, but there are enough wheels turning to recognize a possible message from the great beyond.

"RE-ow." Feed me.

Oh brother. "When I reference messages from the great beyond, Pyewacket, I'm in no way referring to your dietary requirements." I stifle a chuckle as my light-grey eyes roll heavenward.

"Reeeee-ow." A warning. He flicks his short tail, and his black-tufted ears lie back against his broad skull.

"I wouldn't test him if I were you, dear. That caracal without his morning Fruity Puffs is almost as ornery as my granddaughter without her first cup of coffee."

The ominous cloud that haunted my waking moments lifts instantly. "Grams! I don't know what you're talking about. I'm an absolute joy 24/7."

I share a brief giggle with the ghost of my dearly departed grandmother, but she grows quiet and drifts toward the large 6 x 6 windows which offer a view of the great lake nestled in Pin Cherry's harbor. "I felt it too, sweetie."

"Wait, what? I thought you only had visions or visual premonitions. Are you telling me you've suddenly become posthumously clairsentient?"

Grams hovers in front of the panes of slumped glass, and sunlight filters through her translucent form. When I take in her pulled-together, thirty-five-year-old appearance, I almost forget she was in her sixties when she passed. Myrtle Isadora chose a ghost-age that suited her, and I've grown accustomed to it. Her burgundy silk-and-tulle Marchesa burial gown positively glows, and the many jewels draped around her neck and adorning her fingers glisten with mesmerizing twinkles. But she seems far away, lost in memory.

"Are you sure you weren't just reading my thoughts, despite our strict rules to the contrary?"

Ghost-ma waves her bejeweled hand dismissively and arches a perfectly drawn brow. "Who knows? It all gets jumbled up sometimes."

"I'm well aware. That's why we have the handy-dandy rule. If these lips aren't moving, it's none of your business! No thought-dropping. No exceptions."

Pyewacket interrupts my tirade as he launches off the thin summer comforter and stretches lazily on the thick Persian carpet, in a pose carefully referred to as downward "D," to prevent feline wrath. For a moment I toy with the idea of saying the "D" word out loud, just to mess with him.

Grams mumbles, "Someone certainly needs her coffee today."

Without sinking to her level, I stride across my wonderful apartment and press the twisted ivy medallion that opens the secret bookcase door to my hidden quarters.

Pye bursts through the widening gap, hitting my leg with enough force to knock me off balance.

Lurching forward, I catch myself on one of the meticulously aligned oak reading desks and grab the brass lamp for fear it will tip over and shatter the vintage green-glass shade. Such a catastrophe in the Rare Books Loft would not escape the all-seeing eyes of my volunteer employee, Twiggy.

Granted, she's currently in Canada collecting

some rarified tomes that recently came on the market due to the passing of a prominent collector. However, no matter how carefully I cleaned up the mess, she would somehow know what I had done the instant she walked in the door. This constant affirmation of her superior knowledge, and front row seats to my disaster-filled life, are all the payment she requires.

Approaching the wrought-iron spiral staircase, a touch of mischief blossoms. I wind my way down the steps and, when I reach the last stair, I grasp the chain fastened across which displays the "No Admittance" sign, unhook it, and smile proudly.

Twiggy's out of town for an entire week! I'm going to leave that chain unhooked and save myself from the inherent risks in climbing over it every time I need to go up and down the staircase.

I traipse through the stacks toward the back room, slide out the keypad next to our ancient computer, and type in the handy eight-digit code to deactivate the alarm. A deactivation message is not my reward. Instead, the requisite thirty-second window closes and the alarm sounds.

What the . . . I know I typed in the code correctly!

Pyewacket caterwauls and bolts toward the heavy metal door leading to the alley.

I can hardly blame him. If I had to choose between breakfast inside the world's loudest bookstore or starving outdoors in silence, I'd make the same choice. "Here ya go, buddy."

He darts past me and disappears down the alley. I'm sure he'll find something to tide him over until I can pour his precious sugary children's cereal.

"Mitzy! What's going on? Has there been a break-in?"

Covering my ears, I shout to be heard. "Nothing that dramatic." Actually, I don't even have to speak to be heard. Think it, and she will hear. *Grams, I'm authorizing telepathic communication!*

She nods officially and pops a sarcastic salute in my direction.

Taking another stab at entering the elusive code proves fruitless. Any second now my cell phone is going to buzz and the extremely perturbed voice of Twiggy will dress me down and explain to me exactly where I've gone wrong.

Shockingly, my phone doesn't ring. And here I was, thinking I was, like, a psychic or something.

"You need to calm down and focus, Mitzy. Can't you use your gift to see the code?"

Grabbing two fistfuls of my snow-white hair, I thought-scream my retort. *I know the code, Grams. It's not working!*

Before I have a chance to try the code a third

time and hope it's the charm, there's a loud knock at the alley door.

Oh no! The security company must've called the alarm in to the sheriff's station! Hold on, that's not bad news. That's great news! If my tall, blond, and handsome boyfriend, Sheriff Erick Harper, is here to save the day—that works for me.

I kick out a hip, throw open the door, and choke on my sassy intro line. "Deputy Candy?"

The hesitation before he responds makes my skin crawl a little. He may be wearing mirrored sunglasses, but as sure as I'm breathing I know the brown eyes lurking behind those shades are sweeping over my body. "Good morning, Miss Moon."

This *Doogie Howser* of the local sheriff's department is a paltry substitute for my knight-in-shining-armor sheriff. These boyish blond curls and sparse mustache hold no power over me. I'm a "pomade and a clean shave" girl, thank you very much. Arranging my body in a protective stance, I cross my arms and frown. "What are you doing here?"

"Responding to the alarm, Miss Moon. What triggered it?"

I step back and gesture for him to enter the bookstore. "I unhooked the chain at the base of the spiral stairs. But I'm not sure what you plan to do, because I've already tried the alarm code three times, and it's not working!" Actually, I only tried it twice, but three sounded better in my rant.

"Not a problem. Do you have a landline?"

Listen to this kid. He's supposed to be some nineteen-year-old super genius who graduated from high school and college early, only to take his brilliance to the law enforcement academy, and he asks if an old bookstore in a town that tech forgot has a landline? Gimme a break! "This way." I cover my ears with my hands and lead him to the phone in the back room.

Deputy Candy picks up the receiver and punches in a number. "Yes, this is Deputy Candy of the Birch County Sheriff's Department responding to the alarm at the Bell, Book & Candle Bookshop on First Avenue and Main Street."

He pauses for additional questions.

"Correct. There is no intruder, and no emergency in progress. It's a false alarm." He looks at me and lifts his brow for confirmation.

I nod affirmatively.

"Yes. Badge number 762. Yes, I will hold."

He tilts his head toward me and slides his sunglasses down his nose. "They're going to confirm my badge through county dispatch, and then we can reset the code. They'll need a new authentication password."

"Marchesa. M-A-R-C-H-E-S-A." I'm not sure

why I went with that word, but it seems like one of the better options. It's not a name anyone would directly associate with me, or a known birthdate.

He nods, grins slyly, and pushes up his shades. "You should hook that chain, so they can reset the system."

Something about this kid . . . I don't like it. Truth be told, the alarm is stabbing into my last nerve, and that could be clouding my judgment. As I march toward the "No Admittance" chain, I can still hear him on the phone.

"Correct. I'm here with the owner, Mizithra Moon."

It shouldn't surprise me he knows my legal name, but it only adds to the creep factor.

He gives them the new password and they issue a new alarm code. He loudly repeats it to me as he types it in the keypad.

Finally the deafening bells and sirens are silenced.

My ears are still ringing, and I tip my head from side to side, hoping to dislodge the temporary tinnitus on my return trip to the back room.

"Anything else I can help you with this morning?" He takes a step toward me. I step to the side of one of the wooden chairs and casually pull it between us. "Nope. Thanks."

He licks his lips, grins, and walks out.

Before he makes it two strides, Pyewacket appears from nowhere and takes a deadly swipe at his ankle.

"Ow! That thing is dangerous!" Candy rubs his ankle, frowns, and stalks to his car.

Whispering to my heroic feline, I can't help but grin. "Good work, Pye." An unexpected visit from the creeptastic Candy must've been the source of my unsettling premonition this morning.

As far as I'm concerned, there's no better way to remove the stain of unwanted man-child than with a heaping helping of Erick Harper. Firing off a quick text, I invite my boyfriend for a late breakfast at my favorite diner.

Much to my delight, my phone pings with a nearly instant reply. "Breakfast? At 10:30 a.m.? I wish I was an heiress."

I fire off my reply just as speedily. "Rude."

His reply is brief, but promising. "Short-handed. Time for coffee and a doughnut. See you in 10?"

I weigh the obvious quips about cops and doughnuts and instead raise the bar on his challenge as I type. "Make it 5, copper."

Racing up the stairs, I pull the candle handle next to my precious copy of *Saducismus Triumphatus*, and peel off my oversized sleep shirt as the bookcase door slides open.

"Where are you headed in such a hurry?" Grams' knowing smirk gives her away.

"I don't have time for your foolish questions, woman. I've gotta make it to Myrtle's Diner in five minutes!"

Ghost-ma chuckles. "In my day, women used to take their time getting ready and men understood they were worth the wait."

As I squeeze into my skinny jeans, I spout my defense with some difficulty. "As my favorite modern-day philosopher Ferris Bueller says, 'Life moves pretty fast.'"

She shakes her head and morphs through the wall rather than watch my pitiful efforts.

I rifle through the small pile of T-shirts on the floor of my extravagant *Sex and the City* meets *Confessions of a Shopaholic* closet and finally find what I'm looking for. A green tee with a bowl of lettuce and the phrase, "This salad tastes like I'd rather be fat."

When I emerge, my resident ghost stylist tosses in her two cents. "Oh, Mitzy, you're such a hoot. And I admire your 'devil may care' attitude. I suppose when I was your age it didn't take much to transform me from a lump of coal into a diamond."

I glance at her ring-ensconced fingers and roll my eyes. "Looks like you were transformed into a diamond several times, Myrtle Isadora Johnson Linder Duncan Willamet Rogers."

She ignores my jab at her laundry list of former husbands. "You be sure to give Odell a special 'hello' for me."

Since I'm currently splashing water on my face, a nonverbal reply is my easiest bet. *We both know it would absolutely break Odell's heart to think that your ghost was just a couple of blocks away and he had no way to communicate with you. Let him hold your memory in his heart and continue to visit your grave every year. That's how normal people deal with death.* I rake my fingers through my hair and blot the dripping water off my face before racing out of the apartment.

The persistent apparition follows me down the stairs. "At least say hello to Erick. He knows about me now. And I'm sure he's wondering what I've been up to."

Stepping into the alley, I call out, "You're a legend in your own mind, Grams!"

The metal door slams behind me and, not for the first time, I'm pleased that her spirit is tethered to my bookshop and can't continue her self-indulgent rant down Main Street.

Humidity hangs heavy in the air. The crisp wind I imagined this morning is nowhere to be found. There's barely a ripple on the surface of the massive body of freshwater just beyond the cul-de-sac next my bookshop.

I hate to run in this heat, but a bet's a bet.

Pushing through the door, I step triumphantly onto the black-and-white vinyl flooring inside the diner named after my grandmother, and look to the corner booth.

Erick comically pantomimes stopping the timer on his phone and shakes his head. "Bad news, Moon. Five minutes, seventeen seconds. I think we said loser buys breakfast?"

Hurrying toward him, I lean across the red-vinyl bench seat and plant a good morning kiss on his eager lips. "I don't think we decided on consequences, but I'm happy to support local law enforcement and their doughnut addiction." All right, I couldn't resist the obvious punchline forever.

He grins, and I turn to wave at my surrogate grandfather behind the grill. Odell offers his standard spatula salute through the red-Formica-trimmed orders-up window as I slide onto the seat beside Erick.

As usual, there's no need for me to place an order. Odell Johnson always knows exactly what his regulars need, which allows me to focus all my attention on the delicious dish right beside me. "In your text you said you were shorthanded. Is that why you sent Deputy Candy to respond to the alarm code?"

Erick scrunches up his face and shakes his head. "Alarm code? What are you talking about?"

The tightly wound, flame-red bun of the world's best waitress temporarily dips in front of us as Tally slides steaming cups of black gold onto the table. She smiles politely and slips away to attend to the smattering of other customers.

"I set off the alarm at the bookshop this morning, and the code wasn't working. Twiggy's in Canada, and, shockingly, didn't call to reprimand me. I guess the alarm company must've called the sheriff's station, and that's why Deputy Candy showed up at my doorstep."

Erick takes a sip of his coffee and lets out a little murmur of pleasure before he replies. "Hm, I didn't hear anything come over the radio, but I was buried in paperwork, and I guess I could've missed it. Everything okay?"

"Aside from the residual ringing in my ears, yeah. He called the alarm company and they reset the passcode. I'm sure Twiggy will be all kinds of irritated with me when she gets back, but that's future me's problem."

He walks his hand down the table toward me and turns his palm up. As I slip my hand into his, he asks, "I meant, was everything okay with Candy?"

"Oh. I don't know. The guy gives me the creeps, all right? I know there's not really any logical explanation; it just is what it is. But as long as there are no more surprises today, I think I'm fine." A long satisfying sip of java bolsters my hopes.

Odell delivers a freshly warmed cinnamon sticky bun to the sheriff and the standard scrambled eggs with chorizo, golden home fries, and a bottle of Tabasco to me. He places a hand on my shoulder. "I went by the library construction site. Your foundation is doing a heckuva job to put things right after that tornado. Like I always say, this town was lucky to have Isadora, and they're doubly lucky to have you."

His kind words warm my heart. I glance up into his well-lined face and smile with gratitude. "I'm happy to help. Pin Cherry Harbor is the first place since— Never mind. It feels like home."

He scrapes his fingers through his utilitarian grey buzz cut, ignores my almost comment about my deceased mother, and smiles. "You goin' to the bake-off?"

I shrug and glance from Erick back to Odell. "Bake-off?"

"The Pin Cherry Harbor pie-baking contest at the county fair. Winner gets bragging rights for a full year—not to mention prime real estate at the Pin Cherry Festival." Odell raps his knuckles twice on the silver-flecked white Formica table and returns to the kitchen.

A flashback paints my cheeks as red as pin cherries. Thankfully, Erick lets sleeping dogs lie, and neither of us mentions my first visit to the Pin Cherry Festival. That's definitely another story.

As I dig into my delicious breakfast, the sound of air brakes draws my attention beyond the diner's window. A large bus stops across the street opposite Myrtle's.

Memories and emotions flood over me. I remember stepping off that bus with nothing more than a backpack and a manila envelope. Well, there was also a ton of cash shoved in my bra and shoes, and the strange triangular brass key dangling from a chain around my neck, but . . .

I had no idea what I would discover in Pin Cherry Harbor when I climbed on that cross-country bus from Arizona. In fact, if I hadn't caught sight of Myrtle's Diner and stumbled across the street to sample the french fries, Erick Harper might never have fallen for me. And when I say fall, I mean literally. He tripped, he fell, and I landed right on top of him.

Before I can pull Erick down memory lane with me, the bus drives away and leaves a lone figure standing on the sidewalk. The man looks up and down the street with familiar confusion. His eyes track to the diner's neon sign and he smiles as he steps off the curb.

There's something familiar about that grin. I bolt out of the booth and press a hand to either side of my face. "Ben?"

The door swings open, and the lean, muscular man steps inside.

"Shady Ben!"

CHAPTER 2

WITHOUT THINKING, I rush across the diner and throw my arms around his neck.

He returns the embrace, pulls back, and attempts to follow up with a kiss.

I stumble backward, suddenly very aware of my surroundings, and the uninvited audience. "What are you doing up here? Why are you in Pin Cherry?"

He smirks and pushes up one side of his dark mustache with the back of his finger. "I thought it was going to be a lot harder to find you, Mitz. Can't believe you still call me Shady Ben. You'd break my *abuela's* heart."

My cheeks flush. "Old habits die hard, Alvarez. Seriously, what the heck are you doing in almost-Canada?"

His shoulders relax, and his laughter fills the small diner. "No doubt. No doubt. I went through so many states, I lost track. But I had to see for myself, you know?"

"Actually, I don't. What is it that you had to see for yourself?"

"Oh, right." Holding up his hands in mock surrender, he shrugs playfully. "I ran into Dean. You know, your old SUPER-visor at Hot Kafka? He said you'd been in town and you had money and stuff."

While I appreciate him emphasizing the "super" since Dean was never short on being *super* pumped or *super* concerned, I don't like the implication behind Ben's visit. "So you spent the last forty-plus hours on a bus just to see if I had money?"

He laughs, lifts his marred fists in a teasing rope-a-dope, and makes another attempt to kiss me.

Once again, I dodge his advance.

"Come on, Mitz. What gives? Why you acting all bajiggity? You know you owe me some serious green, right?"

This suddenly feels like the type of discussion one doesn't have in the middle of a diner. A self-conscious flood of reality washes over me, but before I can set things right, a familiar voice intrudes.

"This guy bothering you?"

Shady Ben takes one look at the sheriff's uniform and stumbles backward. "Hey, man, I'm not looking for any trouble. She's an old friend, that's all. No stress. No stress, okay."

After a gulp of air and a difficult swallow, I attempt to smooth things over. "Benicio Alvarez, meet my boyfriend Erick Harper."

The color drains from Ben's face, and then he bursts out laughing. "Good one, Mitz. Man, you got me. You got me good." He points at me with one hand and thumps his chest with the other in an attempt to catch his breath. "For reals, though, what'd you do? Can't be parking tickets. This babe can't afford a car."

Erick chews the inside of his cheek and glances at me expectantly.

"Why don't you join us for breakfast, Ben. I'll get you up to speed. Cool?"

His eyes bounce from me to Erick and back to me like a tennis ball at Wimbledon. "Sure, yeah. Sounds good."

We head to the booth, and Tally slides another cup of coffee onto the table, but she offers me an unusually harsh stare before she sweeps away.

"So, they got menus in this *Pleasantville* place, or what?"

You guessed it! I met Ben at film school. He finished, I dropped out. "Don't worry about it. You'll get what you need."

He shrugs and leans forward. "You've changed, Mitz. I can't put my finger on it, but something about you is different. You look different." He leans back and shakes his head.

Erick slips an arm around my shoulders and gives me a squeeze. "I think you'll find that look is happiness, Ben."

Yeesh! Two minutes into this horrifying triumvirate and we've already reached the posturing stage. I twist toward Erick and offer a pleading smile. "Look, Benicio is an old friend and you're my boyfriend. Let's not stir up trouble where there isn't any." Turning back, I throw Erick a little side-eye and he nods once. "So, how long will you be in town, Ben?"

"Are you serious right now? You're, like, living here? Permanently?"

My spine straightens with unspoken offense. "Yeah. Pin Cherry Harbor is my home. I own a business, I have employees—I'm part of the community." The *employees* thing may be an exaggeration, but he doesn't need to know that.

Ben leans back, whips his long black bangs to the side, and groans as though someone knocked the wind out of him. "Whoa! You're serious. What happened to my party girl? What happened to the old Mitz?"

"She grew up. She found her family." I stare

daggers into his dark eyes, and he's the first to look away.

Ben looks down and rubs his thumb along the edge of the table. "Yeah, I guess there was nothing keeping you in Arizona, you know?"

I'm sure he thought the comment would draw out some long-buried emotions, but the truth is I don't think I ever felt the same way about Benicio as he felt about me. In case it's not crystal clear, my life in Sedona, Arizona, was a wreck. I successfully ran away from the last of nearly a dozen foster homes at the age of seventeen and I took whatever opportunities came my way to earn some money and survive. I'll be the first to admit that I may have taken advantage of my relationship with Ben and used his feelings to my benefit. Present-day Mitzy feels bad about that abuse of the friendship, but back in the day my life literally depended on it. All I can do now is attempt to set things right. "Things were different back in Arizona, Ben. You know what my life was like. You were definitely a better friend to me than I was to you."

His big puppy-dog-brown eyes look up at me with disappointment. "Just friends, huh? You really have changed, Mitz."

Odell slides a plate in front of Ben and walks back to the kitchen without a word.

Ben looks at me accusingly. "Did you tell him?"

Glancing at the fried-egg sandwich, four sausage links, and double helping of hash browns, I grin. "Nope. He has a gift." I slide the bottle of Tabasco toward Ben.

"Thanks."

I chuckle as he dives into the delicious offering.

Erick clears his throat and waves a hand to Tally. "I better take this to go, Mitzy. I'm pretty swamped today, but I can bring dinner over tonight."

Sliding out of the booth, I plant an over-eager kiss on Erick's unsuspecting lips and blush self-consciously. "I'm gonna show Ben around town today, and take him to dinner."

Erick's jaw clenches, but to his credit he doesn't protest—directly. "The Harbor Motel always has vacancies and they're reasonably priced."

Tally leans across the table, grabs the cinnamon roll, and boxes it up for the sheriff.

Crossing my arms, I offer Erick half a smile. "Oh, the Harbor Motel has vacancies, does it? I'll be sure to get a room there for Mr. Alvarez. Should I drop your name with the *maître d'* to get a discount?"

Erick scoffs under his breath, accepts the to-go bag from Tally, and tips his head toward me in that way that insinuates a hat. "See you for breakfast, Moon."

As I slide back into the booth, the antique mood ring on my left hand tingles and I glance down as an image of handcuffs wavers deep within the smoky-black cabochon. No idea what that means. Maybe it's just some weird symbol referencing Erick's reluctance to leave me to my own devices with Ben.

Time to take a page from my grandmother's Alcoholics Anonymous handbook and make amends. "Beni, I'm sorry I took advantage of our friendship. I honestly forgot how many times you bought my drinks, or loaned me a little cash at the end of the month, or shared your dinner with me. You were a good friend. Actually, a great friend. I'm not gonna apologize for the state of my life back then. I was lucky I survived at all. But I recognize that a portion of that survival is thanks to you. I hope you'll let me attempt to make up for all of that today. Pin Cherry really is an awesome town. I'd be happy to show you around, and I'm equally happy to pay back the money I owe, if that's all you actually wanted."

Ben leans back in the bench seat and spreads his arms, like Jesus in the da Vinci painting of *The Last Supper*. "I didn't travel halfway across the country for money, Mitz. But I should've realized that if you hadn't reached out in almost two years, there'd be a reason. Looks like that reason's name is Erick Harper."

He's not wrong. "Things with Erick and I have

only gotten serious quite recently. I honestly stayed in this town for a lot of other reasons." One of those biggest reasons would be the ghost living in my bookstore, but I can't exactly share that detail with Ben.

"Hey, I get it, Mitz. You don't owe me any kind of explanation. We were friends. I get that now." A stormy look grips his face and he shoves food roughly into his mouth.

"Don't be like that, Beni. I was a mess, all right? We were probably more than friends, but I couldn't admit it to myself at the time. Let me make it up to you."

He leans forward. "That sounds interesting." His dark eyes twinkle and he reaches a hand across the table.

As I lean away, the hawk-eyed gaze of Odell pricks my clairsentience with disapproval. I gaze toward the proprietor and smile and nod. Just like my mama always told me. "Look, Ben, we're friends. Maybe we were more than that in the past, but not now. What I have with Erick is something I've been waiting for all my life. I'm not gonna screw it up. I've screwed up way too many things and I might've finally learned my lesson. Let me show you around, put you up at the motel, and pay for your ticket back to Sedona."

"That's it? Show me around and buy me a one-way ticket out of town?"

"You said it yourself, Ben. It's been two years. What did you expect?"

He nods and rubs the edge of his mustache with his knuckle. "You're right. Let's see this town that captured the heart of Arizona's last party girl."

"Oh brother. Exaggerate much?"

We share a tension-breaking chuckle, finish our breakfasts, and head out for a day of sightseeing.

CHAPTER 3

As WE STEP onto the sidewalk, Ben gestures down
Main Street. "What happened to this place? Why
are so many of the businesses boarded up?"

"I'm no expert, but I heard that the town was
booming back in the heyday of the iron-ore mines.
Once the mines shut down, the town nearly col-
lapsed. It was only through the quick thinking of
the Chamber of Commerce that they were able to
reposition Pin Cherry as a premier tourist destination." I leave out the details of how my Grampa
Cal's money and my grandmother's donations to
the historical society funded most of the gentri-
fication.

He lifts a brow and smiles. "So what I'm
looking at is considered success?"

The love of my new hometown has probably

clouded my judgment. When I imagine it through Ben's eyes, it takes a different tack. "Maybe boutique destination is a better phrase. However, for the businesses that stayed afloat and the folks who call this place home, it's a rousing success."

He rubs his hands together expectantly. "So, where are you taking me first?"

"First stop: my bookstore."

He nods and falls in step beside me as I head toward the Bell, Book & Candle Bookshop.

"What do you know about running a bookstore?"

The question brings an uncontrollable snort as I shake my head. "Practically nothing. Luckily I have a great employee, who used to work for my dearly departed grandmother. Unfortunately, she's traveling this week and you won't have a chance to meet her." Despite what I said to Ben, Twiggy being out of the country is extremely fortunate.

"Grandmother?" He shakes his head in disbelief.

"Trust me, I was as shocked as you are. That's what actually brought me up here in the first place. I inherited some stuff, so I came to check it out. Once I got here, and met my dad, I couldn't see much reason to leave."

Ben stops in the middle of the street, grips my elbow, and turns me toward him. "Your dad? I thought your dad was dead? So you're not an orphan?"

"I know, right? Actually, before we head into my bookstore, there, let me walk you over to the Duncan Restorative Justice Foundation and I'll introduce you to my father."

Ben shuffles alongside like a dazed sleepwalker. We enter the foundation and pause in the grand lobby to admire the original terrazzo floors, ornamental plaster cornices, and marble walls surrounding the elevator bank.

"See that statue? That's my grandfather." I toy with the idea of telling him about the murder accusations that initially kept me in town, but that's another story.

"Mitzy!" My dad waves his powerful arm as he descends the last few stairs, strides across the lobby, and wraps me in a bear hug. "Perfect timing, but to what do I owe the pleasure?" He narrows his grey eyes and glances questioningly at Ben. "Client or friend?"

The question leaves me at a loss for words, and Ben is forced to introduce himself.

"Benicio Alvarez. I was, um, friends with Mitzy back in Arizona." He shakes my father's hand and asks, "So you work here? Like a manager or something?"

Jacob grins and pats Ben firmly on the shoulder.

"Name's Jacob Duncan. I started this foundation and built this place after a fire destroyed the original building."

"Duncan?" Ben casts a confused glance my way. "I thought your last name was Moon, Mitz?"

My father bites his lower lip and shakes his head of bone-white hair—an exact match for my own.

"Moon was my mother's last name. They never married. In fact, my dad didn't really know about me—technically."

Ben waves his hands and leans back. "Hey, sorry. I got my own weird family stuff. No judgment. Just glad you reconnected, or whatever. Mitzy is a good kid."

I punch him on the shoulder and he hops onto his back foot like the prize-winning middleweight boxer he used to be. Teasingly, I growl and put up my dukes. "Kid? Who are you calling kid, punk?"

He dances his weight back and forth and chuckles. "I don't know. I'm trying to shift gears, you know?"

Even though I know exactly what he's talking about, having this "we used to be friends with benefits but now we're just friends" conversation in front of my dad is not going to happen. "I'm going to show Ben around town. Do you think Stellen would want to come with us?"

Jacob shakes his head. "Amaryllis and Stellen left yesterday afternoon. After his orientation trip to the dorms last month, he felt that there were gonna be too many distractions involved with living on campus. They headed down to find some appropriate off-campus housing before everything gets snapped up. You know Amaryllis. She'll make sure that young man is organized within an inch of his life."

Reaching out, I place a hand on my father's shoulder and we both laugh. My stepmom and my adopted brother are a dynamic duo. She's a shrewd lawyer with a big heart, and he's a dedicated student with a passion for helping animals. I'm sorry he won't be able to join us today, because I really could have used a buffer. "That's all right. We'll manage on our own. Any highlights that an old-timer like you would classify as 'don't miss'?"

"Old-timer?" My father feigns a moment of offense, but smiles broadly. "If the weather holds, you could always jump on the boat and take him out to lunch at Chez Osprey. You know where I keep the keys."

"Thanks, Dad. We'll see what kind of trouble we can get into in town, but I'm sure we can squeeze that into our packed itinerary."

Ben's expression is a mixture of awe and disbelief. "So, when Dean said you had money and stuff, that was like the understatement of the century."

Jacob slings an arm around my shoulders and smiles. "We both ended up with more than we deserve. My story is a lot longer than Mitzy's. But if you buy her a plate of french fries, she'll tell you everything. You guys have a great day. I've gotta drive down to the penitentiary and speak on behalf of a couple guys coming up for parole. We'll have lunch later in the week, okay?"

"You bet. Good luck, Dad." I can only imagine how difficult it will be for him to walk back through the gates of the penitentiary where he spent fifteen years for a crime he mostly didn't commit. But the fact that he's doing it tells me I come from excellent stock. If he can turn a dark past into a bright future, I can make things right with Ben. "Come on, Beni. Let the adventures begin!"

Leading him out the alley door of my father's place, across said alley, and through the side door of my bookshop takes no time at all. Once inside, I lead him into the center of the first floor, where time seems to stand still.

Ben turns in a slow 360 degrees before leaning back and drinking in the tin-plated ceiling and enormous chandelier. "Holy *NeverEnding Story*, Mitz. All this is yours?"

A whoosh above his head grabs my attention.

Isadora is among us. "Not entirely! Feel free to tell him that your generous grandmother deserves most of the credit."

It appears Grams and her thought-dropping are winning all hands in today's game of psychic poker. *Zip it, Grams. Ben is an old friend from Arizona, and I plan on hustling him out of town first thing tomorrow. The last thing he needs is a set of ghost chills to give him an intriguing reason to hang around.*

"Have it your way, dear. I'll be working on my memoirs. So if you're determined to keep me a secret, don't take him to the third floor."

"Hey, you in there? Did that slight breeze blow your focus? I remember the way you used to space out sometimes, but this one was almost like you were in another dimension."

My loud, forced laughter grates on my ears. "Hilarious. I was wondering if we should make a pass through the museum, but that seems kind of boring. Let me run upstairs and grab some cash, and we'll drive down to the marina. You all right with boats, or should I see if I have some seasickness pills?"

He leans forward with a hand on one thigh and pretends to struggle for air. "Museums, marinas, and Mitzy Moon! Three things I never imagined in the same sentence." He shakes his head and straightens. "My pops used to have an old houseboat on Lake Powell. Pretty sure I can handle it. Are you gonna show me your apartment?"

Cautiously climbing over the "No Admittance" chain at the base of the spiral staircase, I give him a stern look. "Hard pass. Wait here. I'll be right back."

I barely have the wad of cash shoved in my front pocket when a nasty hiss and a decidedly un-manly scream echo up from the stacks.

Running against my will for the second time today, I skid to a stop at the top of the stairs. "Pyewacket! Ben is cool. Do not eat him."

Ben is standing on an over-stuffed ottoman, pressing himself against the end of the bookcase marked "Self-help." I'm powerless to suppress the raucous laughter that escapes.

"Not funny, Mitz. That beast thought it was snack time. I ain't that kinda snack."

Sauntering down the stairs, I offer an additional defense of my half-wild beastie. "Pyewacket is a somewhat domesticated caracal. He prefers Fruity Puffs to human flesh, and he is all snarl and no sting."

He tentatively steps down from the footstool and takes several shallow breaths. "He looks dangerous."

"Oh, he looks dangerous, but as long as you

don't try to touch him or eat his favorite cereal, you should leave with all your fingers intact."

"Yeah, let's go."

"Ready for your breakfast, Pye?"

"Reow." Can confirm.

Ben stands stark still, while I walk to the back room and pour Pyewacket a bowl of sugary children's cereal. Crouching down next to the caracal, I keep my hands to myself as I whisper, "He's only here for one day. Try to be nice. And apologize to Grams for me. See you tonight." Forgetting my manners, I reach out to scratch between his ears, and receive a warning thwack from his right front paw. Luckily, he kept the needle-sharp claws retracted. I should know better than to mess with him when he's eating. That's on me.

"Let's go, Ben. We've got a lot of harbor to cover."

CHAPTER 4

FOR A HOT MINUTE I consider driving the Mercedes to the marina, but Ben's head is already spinning. No need to completely separate it from his body. I flip open the keypad for the Jeep's garage, and tap in the code.

Nothing happens.

"Oh yeah, new code." I close my eyes and quickly replay this morning's code-reset memory with psychic enhancement. Punching in the new code, I step back as the door trundles upward.

Ben glances at the Jeep and scoffs. "An old SUV? I expected a Lotus or possibly a Jaguar."

Shrugging, I ignore his comment and mentally pat myself on the back for avoiding the silver 1957 Mercedes 300SL coupe with gullwing doors.

While driving toward the marina, I make an

offhand mention of the casino off in the distance. As I hoped, Ben has no interest. Even without extrasensory perception I could've predicted that someone who grew up pinching pennies, like me, wouldn't have much interest in gambling.

As we stroll down the dock, I gesture toward the Duncan family yacht. "There she is. The *Tax-Seavasion!*"

He lifts a hand to shade his eyes and whistles loudly. "So, this is yours?"

"Not exactly. It was my grandfather's, and when he—passed away—he left everything to my father."

"Okay, got it. So your dad's loaded and he, like, sets you up with an allowance or something. Right?"

Ignoring his annoying assumption, I slip the mooring ropes off the cleats and coil them on the deck. "You have permission to come aboard, Alvarez."

He steps onto the deck as I reach under the captain's chair to snag the miniature flotation device that serves as a key ring and start the engines.

Ben looks over the high-end yacht and rubs his hands together. "That must be one heck of an allowance, Mitz."

Time to set Shady Ben straight. "Yeah, about that. My dad's deal is kinda separate from mine. His mom and dad weren't married when she passed. She had worked her way through five husbands at that point, and grandpa Cal was only number three on the list. So she had her own money and stuff, and she left that to me."

"Wow, with each piece of info you add this starts to sound more and more like a telenovela."

I chuckle and ease the *Tax-Seavasion* out of her slip. It's a good thing I skipped over so many of the details. If Ben thinks the story so far sounds like a telenovela, he would flip his beanie if he knew the whole truth!

As we cross the expansive harbor toward Fish Hawk Island, memories— some ugly, some beautiful—wash over me.

"Hey, you seem pretty distracted. Maybe you should let me drive."

I swat his hand away from the steering wheel and shake my head sternly. "Thanks, but no thanks. I have several terrifying mind pictures of your driving skills. If memory serves, one of them involved practically going up on two wheels as you raced around a corner to get me back to work after an extended lunch. Sound familiar?"

His eyes twinkle with the salacious memory, and his lips curl in a flirtatious grin. "Now that you're loaded, I guess you don't have to worry about working minimum-wage jobs like the rest of us peons."

Easing the throttle down, I let the boat bob aimlessly in the beautiful blue as I turn to face my former special friend. "I know you think it's funny, but my life was a giant pile of crap before a lawyer showed up with my grandmother's will. Sure, it looks like I won the lottery, but I lost my mother in the process. If you think all this luxury lets me forget that, for even one day, you couldn't be more wrong."

Unwanted tears cascade down my cheeks. I brush them away and hit the throttle. My passenger is silent for the remainder of the journey.

Pulling the vessel alongside the large dock below Chez Osprey is easier than I expect.

Ben hops to the boards and figure-eights the mooring lines around a new set of cleats. He hangs his head and offers me a hand. "I was outta line, Mitz. Totally outta line."

Allowing him to help me to the dock serves two purposes: it shows that there are no hard feelings, and ensures that I won't fall in the drink.

"Mitzy Moon! Your timing couldn't be better." Nimkii strides down the steps and offers a generous wave. "Welcome to Chez Osprey."

Ben leans toward me and whispers, "If Hervé Villechaize walks out from behind that pine tree and says anything about airplanes, I'm gonna jump in this lake and swim back to shore if it kills me."

I slap him on the back and laugh. "Don't worry, Nimkii may possess his own magical skills with food and horses, but he's no Mr. Roarke. You won't be subjected to the dark side of any fantasies on this island."

Ben drags a hand dramatically across his forehead and chuckles.

"I picked fresh blueberries this morning and my nephew just finished making the venison sausage. Come in! Come in! This one is on the house. I need to try out some new recipes."

My guest looks at me and raises one eyebrow.

"Thank you, Nimkii. I keep telling you any debt you owed my grandfather has been more than paid, but I appreciate your hospitality."

"We are only open for a dinner seating on weekdays, eh? So be patient with an old man as he tries to be a waiter and a cook for your lunch."

"Don't worry, we're not in any hurry. I'm looking forward to sampling your creations."

He shows us to a beautifully appointed table with birch-bark napkin rings, tiny birch-log salt and pepper shakers, and a deer-antler candleholder. "Birch beers all around?"

Ben opens his mouth to protest, and I honestly

know exactly how he feels. "Don't worry, Beni. It's good."

Nimkii smiles, but hovers at the edge of the table. "How is Sheriff Harper?"

It doesn't take a psychic to see the true intention of that question. "The *three* of us had breakfast this morning. Ben's an old friend from Arizona. Just visiting for the day. Benicio Alvarez, meet Nimkii. Owner and operator of Chez Osprey."

Ben reaches out and firmly shakes the Native American man's hand. "Nice to meet you. And if this question is inappropriate, just ignore it, no problem. I'm wondering if this is tribal land?"

Nimkii smiles. "We entertain our fair share of tourists here, Mr. Alvarez. Questions are how we all learn. Education provides a platform for discussion. Your questions are welcome here."

Ben nods self-consciously and places his hands in his lap.

"This island was part of Anishinaabeg ceremonial grounds. My ancestors used to come here in birch-bark canoes and perform rituals for crops, hunting, even rain. The island was initially lost to my people when the settlers came, and that resulted in a lighthouse being built on the far side of the island. However, when I was on the Tribal Council—"

"You were on the Tribal Council? When was this?"

Nimkii's dark eyes sparkle with mischief and he squeezes my shoulder. "When your grandfather was around."

"Oh." I know better than to ask any more questions about that. The more I learn about grandpa Cal's questionable business practices, the less I wonder about my own wayward youth. Sure, my gangster foster brother Jarrell heavily influenced me, but I doubt he planted the seed. It's starting to feel more and more like he simply watered it.

When I drift out of my reverie, I discover I missed the meat of Nimkii's story.

". . . And now my family runs the restaurant and inn."

Ben smiles and nods appreciatively. "Thank you for sharing that with me. Family is everything where I come from. I feel you."

Our host nods his head, and, as he turns to retrieve our birch beers, his long salt-and-pepper braid sways against his back.

"I like that guy. Solid. You know what I mean?" Ben leans back and crosses his arms.

"Oh, for sure."

His lips part in a half grin. "Oh, for sure? Is that something you picked up on the harbor?"

"I suppose it is."

"You've changed, Mitzy Moon. Someone domesticated you."

Without revealing my ability to see ghosts, my super-secret psychic powers, or my extra-curricular sleuthing, I have no argument against Ben's accusation. "Don't jump to conclusions, Alvarez. There's a lot you don't know about me."

Before he can launch into an inappropriate response, our host returns with two frosty birch beers. I lift my bottle and offer a loud toast for Nimkii's ears, and Ben's warning. "To old friends."

"And new adventures." He leans forward, clanks the neck of his bottle against mine, and winks.

Shaking my head, I take a long pull on the refreshing beverage. The subtle hint of wintergreen and mystery is more addictive than I ever imagined.

Ben nods and widens his eyes in surprise. "Not bad, Mitz. I think you're onto something with this."

One course blends into the next as Nimkii graces us with his garden's bounty. Dandelion green salad, with roasted pine nuts, fresh chanterelle mushrooms, and beebalm leaves. A cold honeydew and watermelon soup serves as a palate cleanser before the main is served. When I catch a whiff of the fire-roasted venison sausage, with a side of wild rice, sautéed mushrooms, and blueberries, I know I'm in culinary heaven.

My lunch guest grins from ear to ear and shamelessly talks with his mouthful. "Blueberries and rice! I never would've believed it, but it's absolutely delicious."

I nod and smile as I shove a charbroiled slice of venison sausage into my mouth. "Mmmmm."

Nimkii approaches our table, waits for us to swallow, and steps forward. "How is everything so far? What do you think of my new recipes?"

Ben beats me to the punch. "Between you and me, buddy, this is the best food I've ever eaten. Don't tell my *abuela*. She'd never make me tamales again."

We share a laugh, and I second Ben's praise of the menu. "But you said so far. What does that mean?"

He shakes his finger teasingly. "You are as smart as they say. I have a very special dessert prepared. I hope you saved room."

We nod eagerly, but after our host returns to the kitchen, I place a hand on my belly and groan. "I don't know about you, but I didn't save room for anything."

Ben shakes his head. "Speak for yourself, Mitz. I'm ready to eat whatever this guy puts in front of me!"

"Good. You'll probably have to finish mine."

Nimkii returns with hot mugs of roasted

chicory, a coffee-like beverage, and our breathtaking dessert. He lays a plate in front of each of us, and for a moment we both stare, dumbfounded.

"What is it?"

"It's best if you consume first and ask questions later."

Ben and I exchange nervous glances, pick up our spoons simultaneously, and dig in.

Our host and chef cups one hand inside the other and waits patiently.

The small mound of ice cream easily melts into the delicate berry tart. Each item separately is tasty, but together they create some kind of—epicurean alchemy. Silas will certainly punish me for abusing the term, but there's just no other way to describe the taste revelation happening in my mouth.

Ben's shocked and delighted expression must mirror my own.

Nimkii nods with satisfaction and leans toward the table. "Do you want to know the secret?"

Picking up my napkin, I wipe my mouth and smile. "Yes, and no. All right, my final answer is yes. Not knowing will drive me insane."

The chef's eyes widen. "Ah, perhaps they will put that on your headstone."

His unexpected dry humor hits my funny bone, and I laugh into my napkin until tears leak from the corners of my eyes.

Ben smiles, but without my amateur sleuthing backstory, he hardly sees the hilarity in the comment.

"I won't keep you waiting. I made the ice cream with caramelized deer milk, the tart crust is acorn flour, and the berries are a combination of local blackberry, raspberry, blueberry, and pin cherries."

Ben is speechless.

I'm impressed and concerned. "Deer milk? How does one obtain deer milk?"

The gentle human leans down, and the lines in his face seem more pronounced as he grins with hidden knowledge. "Some secrets must be earned."

"Fair enough. It was absolutely delicious. Top marks on every course. Can we get a couple bottles of water for the trip back? I'd like to show Ben around the rest of Pin Cherry before dark." Reaching into my pocket, I extract a wad of bills and begin smoothing them on the table.

Nimkii pushes the money toward me. "I told you, your money's no good here. You put that toward the library project, or one of your other philanthropic ventures. One good deed deserves another, Miss Moon."

He clears our plates and disappears into his magical kitchen.

Ben's eyes are wide as saucers. "I feel like you're leaving out some of the best parts of your new five-star life, Mitz. Philanthropic ventures? What the heck?"

I brush away his concern with a casual flick of my wrist. "Come on. Let's head back to the mainland, and I'll show you what he was talking about. It's not as grandiose as it sounds."

He follows close behind and mumbles, "Understatement of the century, *número dos*, I'm betting."

CHAPTER 5

HEADING BACK TO THE MARINA, I push the throttle to full. It's a gorgeous day on the massive lake. The fresh air and late summer sunshine are not to be missed. However, I race through the moment because I'm eager to put more activities on the itinerary and avoid additional heartfelt conversations with Ben.

He hangs over the side of the boat and lets the chilly fresh water spray his face as we race across the whitecaps. His wet black hair whips in the wind, and he smooths it backward as he whoops and hollers. "I could get used to this, Mitz!"

Now who's reading minds? Yep, that confirms it. The sooner I return us to a series of mundane tourist traps, the better.

When I guide the boat into her slip at the marina, Ben jumps out and secures the yacht like an expert.

"Next stop: the construction site." Tucking the keys back under the seat, I hop over to the dock with only a momentary wobble.

Ben yanks his T-shirt off over his head and wrings out the water onto the dock. I'm sure I appreciated his lithe frame, taut muscles, and rippling six-pack abs when we were dating, but, if I didn't, I'm happy to sneak a quick peek today. Yes, I'm in a committed relationship with the sheriff, but I'm not blind!

He catches my glance. "I can leave the shirt off if you prefer?"

"Simmer down and put your clothes on. We're going to a library, not a strip club."

He laughs wickedly and slips the damp T-shirt back on. "Food for thought, though."

Rolling my eyes, I lead the way to the Jeep and drive across town in record time. "Here we are."

He leans forward and glances out the front window. "Whoa! You weren't kidding. It's actually a construction site."

"Um, yeah. I'm weird like that. Did you think 'construction site' was a euphemism for something more exciting?"

He shrugs and hops out of the vehicle.

As we approach the single-wide trailer housing

the foreman's office, a familiar harrumph catches my attention.

"Silas Willoughby? Are you taking over the general contractor duties on this project?"

My alchemy mentor and lawyer looks up from the set of blueprints spread across a makeshift plywood table and rubs his sagging jowls. "Mizithra? It's unlike you to move toward the possibility of hard labor."

I throw my hands up in the air in silent protest while he chuckles his way toward me.

At some point he notices the individual next to me. "Are you perchance charging for tours?" Silas smooths his bushy grey mustache with a thumb and forefinger, and his milky-blue eyes methodically scan my sidekick.

"Silas Willoughby, my lawyer, meet Benicio Alvarez, an old friend from Arizona."

Ben eagerly reaches a hand toward the curmudgeon, but Silas takes a moment to straighten his tattered pocket square and fasten one button on his fusty tweed coat before meeting the outstretched hand with his own. "A pleasure to meet you, Mr. Alvarez. Will you be in town long?"

Ben shrugs. "We'll see. I might—"

"Ben's leaving tomorrow. I'm giving him the nickel tour, checking him into the Harbor Motel, and putting him on a plane home tomorrow."

Ben leans back and rubs a hand over his slack jaw. "A plane? I thought you were gonna cheap out and throw me back on that disgusting bus. I should've known a fancy philanthropist would have other plans." He enjoys quite a chuckle at my expense.

Silas ignores the comment and beckons me to follow him toward the blueprints. "The proposal, of course, follows the original plans to the letter. However, the Historical Society has requested an addition on the north side of the new structure."

Nodding my head, I lean down and look at the blueprints as though I understand what I'm seeing. "Doesn't the Historical Society usually veto changes to historical buildings?"

"Indeed. However, in this specific instance they wish to honor your generosity and your grandmother's long-standing patronage with a small museum feature. Half of the museum would contain rotating exhibits pertinent to the interests of bibliophiles. The other half will be a permanent installation honoring the history of the Duncan-Moon family in Pin Cherry."

Drawing up my eyebrows to make room for my widening eyes, I shake my head. "That sounds like a fuse we don't want to light. Felons, alcoholics, bribery—not the museum quality stuff I'd expect."

Silas harrumphs, shakes his head firmly, and his

paunch rises and falls as he exhales a heavy breath of indignation. "My dear Mizithra, the family would have the final say on the items displayed and the narrative provided. I'm sure the Pin Cherry Harbor Historical Society would be far more interested in things like the first railroad spike your grandfather's grandfather's grandfather drove into the Midwest Union Railway, or Sydney Jensen's saxophone, or perhaps the first dollar your grandmother and Odell earned at Myrtle's Diner. Things of that nature would be palatable, would they not?"

Before I have the opportunity to formulate my barely supportive reply, Ben interjects himself into the conversation.

He points to some double lines on the plans. "If you turn this bank of windows into three sets of French doors, they could open onto a patio that might serve some unique local fare, like the stuff we had out at Chez Osprey, or maybe something from the diner. Plus, you could put in a garden, maybe with a statue of Mitzy's grandma. I think a museum sounds cool, Mitz."

Not sure which part shocks me more, the part where Ben takes the museum ideas seriously, or the part where he somehow understands the rows of strange blue lines, boxes, and squiggles on the blueprint. "That's a cool idea, Ben. When did you learn to read blueprints?"

He crosses his arms and strums his fingers on his bicep. "You're not the only one that moved on, Mitzy. I started taking landscape design classes at night school. The film thing is getting me nowhere fast, and I can't see myself struggling to make ends meet with a minimum wage job for the rest of my life."

"Yeah, I get it. Seems like you'll be great at the landscape design stuff. You always had a good eye behind the camera."

He sniffs and lowers his chin like he used to do as he squared off against an opponent in the ring. "Maybe you can put some of that philanthropic money where your mouth is, Mitz. I could use a silent investor in my company."

I had an answer ready. I promise you I did. But my overprotective mentor usurped my opportunity to use it. "The Duncan-Moon Philanthropic Foundation reviews applications monthly. If you care to submit a business proposal, all the necessary forms can be found on the foundation's website."

An odd silence hangs in the air. I'm waiting for Silas to give us the website URL. Because, between you and me, this is the first I've heard of it.

Ben handles the information with more graciousness than I expect. "Thank you, Mr. Willoughby. I'll be sure to check that out."

Silas returns his attention to the blueprints, and

his silence is more dismissive than any farewell he might offer.

"Come on, Beni. I'll take you over to the Midwest Union Railway office. I don't know if you're into old locomotives or not, but there's a pretty sweet old engine in the lobby."

Ben smiles and reaches for my hand. Shoving my hand firmly in my pocket, I walk back to the Jeep and drive the few blocks over.

"What's that place? Final Detination?"

Oh, crapballs. I should've taken the long way around. "It's nothing. Just an old dive bar. There's a letter missing from the sign. It should say Final Destination. Mostly dockworkers and some of the railyard guys. Not much to look at from the outside and even less going on inside."

He stares out the window, and my clairaudience picks up one phrase floating in the ether. "That's the place."

I have no idea what he's thinking about "that place," but it's my intention to keep him otherwise occupied at the rail station. We wind our way through the first floor and he's definitely impressed with the operation. Just when I think we're about to end the tour uneventfully, Anthony Jenkins steps out of the storeroom and waves his arm as though he's signaling an aircraft carrier at sea. "Mitzy! Solve any crimes lately?"

I laugh awkwardly. "Hey, Anthony, glad to see you're still working here."

"Yeah, your dad's the best. Gave me a second, second chance and I'm not about to let him down."

"That's great to hear."

"Who's your friend?" Anthony jerks one of his thumbs toward the stunned man on my left.

"Oh, this is Ben. He's visiting from Arizona."

Ben and Tony quickly pound fists and give each other a patented bro nod. "What's this about Mitzy solving crimes?"

Anthony throws his arms in the air. "Man! I can't believe she's giving you a tour of this dusty place and leaving all the best bits off the roster. She single-handedly caught a notorious train-robbery gang, saved my job, and her dad's business."

Ben pushes at the edge of his mustache and narrows his gaze. "Yeah, funny you didn't mention that, Mitz."

I wave goodbye to Anthony. "Glad to see you're doing the Restorative Justice Program proud." Then I tug Ben by his elbow toward the parking lot. "Give it a rest, Beni. The guy is totally exaggerating. I gave a helpful tipoff to local law enforcement—they did the rest. It was nothing. Let it go."

He digs his hands deep into his front pockets and hunches his shoulders over as he shakes his head. "Sure. Sure. That guy's exaggerating,

Nimkii's making things sound more grandiose than they really are, and Silas has a website set up to accept applications for your philanthropic donations because you're just a small-town girl with a couple extra nickels to rub together. Whatever you say, Mitz. Whatever you say."

Pulling out my phone, I sigh and make a point of checking the time—but my chrono-report is interrupted by a text from Erick.

"Feel free to include the station in your tour. Miss you."

I fire back a quick, "Haha. No time. Headed to motel."

I barely tap the "send" arrow and my phone pings with a reply. "??"

"Get your mind out of the gutter, Sheriff. I'm getting Beni a room."

Ben is trying to look over my shoulder. "Anything I need to know, Mitz?"

Narrowing my gaze, I ignore his question and flick my ringer off. "We better stop at the Harbor Motel and get you checked in before we grab dinner. I don't want the place to fill up and leave you without a place to stay." I hated saying it, but there's no way Ben is going to weasel his way into crashing at my place.

The parking lot at the single-story Harbor Motel couldn't *be* more empty. The only thing missing is a couple of tumbleweeds blowing their way through to really drive the point home.

Ben chuckles smugly. "Yeah, we'll be lucky to get me a room here."

Without bothering to reply, I hop out of the Jeep and march straight into the office. I reserve the room for one night, under Ben's name, and pay cash. The short, squat human on the other side of the dilapidated counter slides me the room key for number fourteen. "Checkouts at 10, not 11."

"Copy that."

Ben hasn't moved from his perch in the passenger seat, and when I hop back into the vehicle, he exhales loudly.

"What are you getting all salty about, Alvarez?"

"Nothing. Just seems like you could've put me up at Chez Osprey for one night and actually let me enjoy this place a little."

The nerve of this guy? I toss him the room key sharply and turn in my seat. "Look, Ben, I didn't ask you to come to Pin Cherry. Frankly, since the minute you got here, all you've talked about is money. Why don't you just tell me exactly how much I owe you? I'll hand over the cash and purchase you a first-class ticket back to 'out of my life.' Sound good?"

His utter silence is unexpected.

My clairsentience takes a direct gut shot, and I notice a tear trickling down his cheek and catching his mustache. "Hey, what's wrong? Are you in some kind of trouble? Why did you really come here?"

He cracks his neck from one side to the other and groans. "I messed up. I messed up pretty bad."

"What do you mean?"

"I finally got a kinda decent gig. A thirteen-episode show. I had all that commercial experience, you know. They made me an assistant to the line producer."

"That sounds great, Beni. Why are you so upset about it?"

"My *abuela's* not doing good."

I'm sure somewhere in his mind these two things connect, but I'm not seeing it. My moody mood ring offers no help, and I'm not picking anything up other than overwhelming guilt. "Tell me what happened."

"She needed cataract surgery. She doesn't have any insurance."

"Weren't they paying you enough on the show? You should've been making good money with a billet like that."

"I wasn't. They were paying me under the table because I got that record."

"What record?"

"I thought I told you 'bout the cars I boosted. That's what got me through film school."

"You boosted cars—plural?"

He shrugs. "I made some decent side-cash, but then I got caught. They only had me on the one, though. I got a suspended sentence and probation." He rubs his mouth. "I'm sure I told you."

"Um, no, you didn't tell me. But I'm starting to figure out how you could afford to finish the program."

"Hey, not everyone can wake up an heiress."

Ignoring the jab, I take the high road. "So what happened on the show?"

"I sorta used some of their money to pay for my *abuela's* surgery. She couldn't even read her recipes, Mitz. What was I gonna do?"

Oh brother. No wonder all he can talk about is money. "Are they looking for you?"

"Looking for me? They're suing me. They're taking me to court to recover the money I stole. I don't have it. I had to pay the medical bills."

"So you came to Pin Cherry because Dean said I had money and stuff. All of this flirting was just some way to get into my bank account?"

He rakes a hand through his long bangs and shrugs. "I thought we had something. It's not like I'm imagining it. I just thought you could help a guy out."

"Hey, I don't appreciate being taken advantage of. There are a lot of things you could've done besides stealing money from your employer. You gotta face the music. It's the only way to put things right."

He leans forward and places both hands on the dash. "I should've known money only flows one way in this relationship. You've changed, Mitz. The old gang would never recognize this straight-laced, uptight chick you've become."

Part of me knows he's still working an angle, but his words hurt. Most of the friendships I had back in Arizona were fake, at best, but how dare he call me straight-laced and uptight. I'm the most laid-back, loose person in Pin Cherry. "Tell you what, Ben. You tell me what I owe you. I'll pay it all back plus interest. And just to show you I'm not uptight, we'll tie one on at Final Destination tonight. Also my treat."

He sniffs and wipes his eyes. "You serious? You're crazy if you think you can drink me under the table, Mitz. I'm still in fighting shape you know."

I start the engine and drive. "Yeah, I'm sure you are, Alvarez. The difference is, I'm also in fighting shape."

He puts a hand over his mouth and whistles. "Oh, snap. That's the bell, folks. Round two."

"I'm ready. You ready?" I clench my jaw. What

if I open old Mitzy's cage and I can't get her back in?

"You good to go with what you're wearing? Maybe you wanna get changed before you buy the first round of shots."

Glancing down at my inappropriate T-shirt, I shrug. "Let's go for it. I'm still full from that massive lunch on the island. I say we have drinks for dinner too."

Ben claps loudly. "Now that's the Mitzy Moon I remember."

I remember her too, and something tells me I'm going to regret bringing her out of retirement.

CHAPTER 6

My BIG MOUTH threw down a gauntlet, but my poor head, and likely my stomach, will end up paying the price. If you thought that my troubles with Ben discovering too much about my new life in this harbor town had ended, you'd be dead wrong. When we open the creaking door and venture into the dark, beer-soaked bowels of Final Destination, the universe has an additional treat in store for me.

The intimidating, barrel-chested owner, Lars, drops the dirty bar rag in his left hand and presses his wide palm to his thick forehead. "Well, if it ain't Daisy!" He pounds his formidable fist on the bubbled varnish and upsets a questionable bowl of stale bar mix as he howls with laughter.

I take a little bow for his amusement and approach one of the multiple empty stools. "Hey, Lars, I know I've apologized before, but let me just throw one more in the mix for good measure. I'm sorry Daisy quit without notice, but it was for a good cause. Right?"

He grabs his best, and only, bottle of tequila and pours three shots. "First round is on the house, and then you start buying them for me."

Ben stands beside an empty stool and stares at me with an unreadable, muddled look.

Lars and I each grab a shot glass and raise it in the air. I throw on my southern accent in honor of the undercover waitress job I took at this establishment on a previous case, and shout, "Drink, darlin'!"

My former employer guffaws and responds, "Down the hatch!"

We each slam our shots and tap our empty glasses twice on the bar.

There's no salt and no limes at Final Destination. You handle your business like a boss, or Lars will tell you where to put it.

"Hey, who's your friend? Some, teetotaler?"

Hoping that I can smooth over all the "Daisy" nonsense, I push the shot of tequila toward Ben. "Come on, Alvarez. This bar crawl was your idea. You better get crawlin' cuz this is the only stop."

He immediately picks up the shot glass, never

breaking eye contact, and drains it dry. He sets it on the bar, shakes his head and mumbles, "I gotta see a man about a horse."

As soon as Ben disappears, Lars leans across the bar with the scowl of an angry parent. "You under cover again? Because if you're stepping out on the sheriff I won't be serving you another drop."

Yeesh! This entire town is Team Erick! "The guy's name is Benicio Alvarez. He's an old friend from Arizona, and he's leaving tomorrow. I promised him a night out on the town and you and I both know there's precious little to choose from in almost-Canada."

Relief melts Lars' harsh expression, and he nods proudly. "I'm sure it goes without saying, Mitzy, but you or Daisy are welcome to work a shift at Final D anytime you want."

I know he means it as a compliment, so I swallow my snarky reply, nod firmly, and smile. "Thanks. How's business been this summer?"

"Well, the fishin' has been the best in a decade, so them city folk are coming up in droves. Seems like my niece set up some kind of Instabook page or some such nonsense and this ol' dive is touted as not to be missed."

The town that tech forgot, indeed. If any of these quaint local businesses had a genuine online presence, our small town charm would disappear over the next four-day weekend. Now that I'm practically a local, I can land firmly on the side of the argument that more tourists means more trouble. "Keep Pin Cherry neat as a pin."

Lars tilts his head and raises a thick blonde eyebrow. "That sounded like a toast. What are you buying me?"

"Set us up with three rum and cokes. I'm a little out of practice, and if I expect to last beyond this next round, I'm gonna have to pace myself."

The lumbering bartender nods once and whips up our drinks as Ben returns.

My old friend slides onto a stool, pulls a bowl of bar mix within his reach and munches silently.

"What's gotten into you? I thought we were tying one on? Remember?"

He shrugs and chomps on his stale pretzels and cheese crackers. "I don't think I can keep up with a celebrity like you, Mitz. Seems like everyone in this town knows you. I feel like an extra quail egg in a nest of fourteen."

For a native Arizonan, the quail reference cuts deep. Those foolish birds lay a ton of eggs, but they don't keep real good track of their offspring. The pile of eggs is simply hedging their bets against predators and possible bird-brained stupidity. I never meant to make Beni feel like an extra egg on that pile. Placing a hand on his shoulder, I give him a stern shaking. "Snap out of it, Beni. This town is about as big as the back of my hand. Everybody knows everybody. And everybody knows everybody's business. If they didn't witness it first hand they read it in the one and only *Pin Cherry Harbor Post*. And I know the guy who owns that too. I'm telling you, small town Sedona is a metropolis compared to this place."

A hint of life seeps back into his eyes, and he almost smiles when Lars serves up our fresh drinks. Lars lifts his rum and coke and says, "Keep Pin Cherry neat as a new pin."

I raise my glass and add, "And to old friends."

Ben slowly hoists his drink in the air and smirks as he adds, "And learning new things!"

We all clink glasses and take hearty gulps of our simple cocktails.

As the rum works its way through my system and joins the fiery tequila already coursing through my veins, I hit the all-important pool-shark phase of my inebriation. At this point, I embody Vinnie from *The Color of Money*.

Strutting my stuff toward one of the pool tables, I feed a bill into the change machine and drop my stack of quarters on the bumper. My cell vibrates in my pocket, but it doesn't take a psychic to figure out Erick is checking up on me again. I'll text him later, when I'm safe and sound at the bookshop. Right now I need to hustle some pool. "You wanna rack 'em or should I, Alvarez?"

Ben slides off the barstool with a chuckle and selects his pool cue from the subpar display.

Lars keeps serving drinks, and my stack of quarters dwindles. The dim light hanging low over the pool table never offered stellar illumination, but the solids and stripes are blurring together. Time to pound a couple of waters and choke down a little stale snack mix.

To be fair, I'm doing better than my opponent. Ben probably weighs less than me, and he suffers from some strange zero-body-fat condition. I've never quite been able to put my finger on what caused it, but it probably had something to do with all the boxing. He's stumbling, I'm mumbling, and it seems like a great time to call it a night.

I proudly toss Lars my keys and announce, with almost no slur, "We're gonna walk it out offside. I'll grab my Jeep wheels in the tomorrow time."

Lars suffers from none of the lack of coordination that haunts me and easily catches the keys. "They'll be here, Daisy. Don't you fret." He nearly chokes on his own laughter, and I steer a lopsided Beni out into the damp night air. Having him hang on me as we stumble down the street is a walk of shame I'm happy no one will witness. At this late hour all the good folk of Pin Cherry are tucked safely in their beds.

When the short whoop of a siren and the flash of red and blue cross our path, even my inebriation can't drown out my embarrassment.

Propping Beni onto his own two feet proves too great a task, and the cruiser's door opens before I can untangle myself.

"I know what you're thinking. It's fine. We're fine." I hope that will soothe Erick's ego.

An unexpected voice calls out. "That's all right. Looks like you two could use a lift."

"Deputy Candy?" The fog in my head is thick, and my psychic senses utterly inaccessible, but it seems like he was on shift first thing this morning. This has to be too many hours. Maybe he's working a double?

While I mentally stumble through timesheet math, Deputy Candy helps me into the back of the cruiser. I fall across the bench seat like it's the Ritz Carlton.

When Candy returns with Ben, there's no room in the back. He opens the front passenger door, and I think there's a sharp yelp as Ben takes his seat. Maybe Ben didn't duck his head like a good little criminal.

The cruiser lurches forward, and before we

make it two blocks, my head swims and I'm out cold.

The dim light of morning feels like daggers in my eyes. I blink and lift my head from a puddle of drool.

Is that a table? This must be a bad dream.

My noggin is swirling, and my stomach is not much better. As I attempt to raise my left hand to wipe the drool from my cheek, I discover two un-nerving things.

One: my left hand is handcuffed to the arm of a wooden chair. You would think that the other alarming thing would be that my right hand is hand-cuffed to the other arm of this chair, but it's going to get much worse before it gets better.

Two: handcuffed beside me, in an identical chair, is Deputy Candy!

My eyes frantically search the unfamiliar room for Ben, but there's no sign of him.

The options seem rather limited. "Candy! Deputy Candy, wake up!"

The young deputy rolls his head from side to side and discovers his predicament in pretty much the same way I discovered mine. "Where'd these handcuffs come from?" He looks at me suspiciously, breathing fast. "Did you do this? Is this some kind of sick joke?"

Frowning, I shake my head and demonstrate my accommodations. "Sure, Candy. I brought you to someplace I've never been, handcuffed you to that chair, and then somehow handcuffed myself to a chair too. Seems like the most logical explanation, wouldn't you say?"

Yes, that was harsh. Try to remember I have a hangover, and I'm in no mood to suffer fools, as Silas would surely say.

The deputy tests the strength of his bonds, checks his shoulder for his duty mic—which is missing along with his gun—and shouts at the top of his lungs.

My pounding headache could definitely have done without that last one. "It seems like we're the only ones here. Do you have any idea where *here* is?"

He looks down at the handcuffs once more and shakes his head. "Your phone. Do you have your phone?"

Straining my fingers to poke at the front pockets of my skinny jeans, I find them empty. I shift my weight back and forth on my ample backside, but feel no phone-shaped object poking me. "That's a big negatory, good buddy. Any other bright ideas?"

He sits back and methodically runs his eyes

over every inch of a room that seems like it popped off the pages of a 1950s *Ladies Home Journal.* "If we go with the obvious, and assume the one person missing is the one who put us here—"

"Beni? You think Ben, the guy who was so drunk he couldn't walk upright, somehow kidnapped both of us and transported us to wherever this is, and took us prisoner in this house! You are either stupid, or insane. At this point I'm not sure which is more terrifying."

His teeth grind together as he clenches his jaw. "Listen, Miss Moon, I'm aware that you're used to having things go your way, but if you'll take a moment to look at that teapot collection on the oak shelves, I think you'll notice that the third teapot in the second row down doesn't look quite right. Someone put us here. And that someone is watching us right now."

My bleary eyes navigate the deputy's angry directions, and I have to agree. The teapot tipped over on its side, with the lid removed, looks like the perfect place to hide a small nanny cam. "So what's the plan? What kind of scheme do you think this person is running? There are no papers here for one of us to write a confession, there are no cue cards directing us to say something that they plan to use against us, and"—this next part is the most terrifying—"there's no food."

Candy glances up and down the kitchen's white Formica counter, edged with aluminum, and nods. "You're right. I don't see any food either. But there's water." He gestures with his chin.

Somehow the glass of water with the convenient bendy straw escaped my notice. Leaning forward, I grip the straw between my lips and drink like an explorer who's stumbled across an oasis in the desert.

"I'd slow down if I was you."

Pushing the straw out from between my lips with my tongue, I suck in a lungful of air, preparing to give this man-child a piece of my mind.

"You can do whatever you want, Miss Moon. I'm just thinking about what will happen if you drink a lot of water right now."

Twisting my wrists in handcuffs, I realize the error of my ways. "Good point. Solid advice, Candy."

"Do you remember anything about how we got here?" He curves his spine painfully and stretches a finger out to rub his nose.

"Not exactly. I remember you stopped to give Beni and me a ride . . . Then I must've passed out. I don't remember anything till I woke up, here, this morning."

Candy nods. "Yeah. I remember picking you guys up. I drove a couple of blocks—then it's all a blank. And the back of my neck itches worse than any mosquito bite I've ever had."

"Let me see."

He cranes his neck forward, and I lean over to get a closer look. There is a tiny puncture mark on the back of his neck, just above his collar. And there even appears to be some slight bruising, as though it was injected with force. "There's some kind of mark." I keep the details to myself.

"See! I'm telling you, that friend of yours was faking the whole thing. Soon as we got in the cruiser, he must have injected me with something. In fact, I remember him pointing off to the left and yelling, 'Look out!' That's probably when he stuck me."

"Why would Ben kidnap a cop?"

"Maybe he only intended to kidnap you. Then I came along and he had to change up his plan."

"All right. And why would he need to kidnap me? We're friends. I was hanging out with him of my own free will."

"Maybe it was ransom money he had in mind."

Those words don't feel good in my ears. Beni had been talking about money ever since he arrived. Once he saw what my family was worth and realized how much the community respected me, I bet he figured he could pay off his grandmother's medical bills, settle his lawsuit, and still have plenty left over to start his landscaping company with a good ol' Duncan-Moon ransom. That is, if anything he told me is even true. Maybe his grandmother isn't sick, and he just got tired of boosting cars. Maybe kidnapping is his new source of income.

"Not so smart now, eh, Miss Moon?"

Of all the people Ben had to trap me with! Why did it have to be Deputy Candy? Why couldn't Erick have been out patrolling the streets?

CHAPTER 7

IF BEN, or whoever kidnapped us, thinks that I'm going to sit around making small talk with Deputy Candy until my bladder reaches a mission-critical state, they don't know whom they're dealing with.

Without warning, I stand up and run backward at full force. The wooden beast of a chair crashes against the counter. My temples pound and there's an audible creak from my uncooperative chair. And nothing more.

Yet another movie trope that disappoints. My solid, probably quarter-sawn oak chair doesn't smash to smithereens like a cheap balsa-wood set piece in every action movie I've ever seen.

"What are you doing? Somebody might come back. What if they have my gun?" Deputy Candy's green roots are showing.

I've been in trouble more times than I care to count, and I've actually gotten myself out one or two of those times. "Let them come. I'm not gonna sit here and starve until some half-cocked psycho decides to pay us a visit."

Candy struggles against his rigid restraints and squeaks. "What about the camera?"

My eyes roll all by themselves. "Look, Candy— Oh, for crying out loud, I can't possibly call you that for heaven knows how long. What's your first name, kid?"

"Lane."

From my hunched over position with a chair basically handcuffed to my back, I don't have far to go to lean over and let loose a massive belly laugh. "Wow! I don't have a great track record with parents or families, but did your parents hate you? Are you gonna sit there and tell me that your name is Lane Candy? As in Candy, Lane on every alphabetical roster in the history of ever?" The laughter grips me again, and the only thing that stops me short is the unknown bathroom component of this kidnapping.

His face scrunches up as though the clever wordplay had never crossed his mind. Maybe it hadn't. You know what they say about geniuses— sometimes they can't see the forest for the trees. All book smart and no street smart. Looks like that's what I'm dealing with, and that means escape will be up to me.

I step forward, brace my manacled hands against the stout wooden table, and shout, "Once more for the cheap seats!" I launch myself backward with renewed force, and two of the chair legs crack. "Yes!"

Candy looks at me and shakes his head in dismay. "I'm not sure what you're so excited about, Mitzy. All you've done is break two legs off the chair. Now you can't sit down, and you have a chair strapped to your back."

"Oh, ye of little faith, Lane." Shambling toward the front door like *The Hunchback of Notre Dame*, I press myself sideways and test the door handle. "Locked. No surprise, but I had to check."

The look on his face is priceless. Not quite sure if it's something he never thought of, or he's simply amused at my "girl in chair" comedy routine.

No time like the present to scout the area.

In addition to the sparse and somewhat outdated farmhouse kitchen, there's a set of stairs leading up, a padlocked door that could lead to a pantry or possibly basement. The idea of a basement never would've occurred to me prior to arriving in Pin Cherry. They're such a rarity in Arizona, I'd never even seen one. However, now that I'm practically a local, the shock has subsided, and it does seem like a logical option. The next room is a large family room with a— "Fireplace!"

I break into a run toward the gorgeous beacon of split rock and hurl myself against it back first.

Success!

The cross bars of the chair split and, with several smaller bashing's against the sharp corner and one or two regrettable seat drops, I'm halfway to freedom.

The left backpost splinters and separates with a satisfying crack, and I'm able to wrench the back from the seat. The remaining two legs and bottom drop to the floor. I kick them angrily across the room as punishment for the trouble they've caused. Now, dangling from each wrist is an arm, and roughly half of the chair back.

Would it shock you to know this isn't my first time in handcuffs? Before I proceed with any more bashing and clambering, I need to wrap something around my wrists to protect them from the inevitable skin breaking friction caused by the unwelcome metal wristbands.

When I return to the kitchen, the deputy's face is a mixture of shock and anger. I can only assume that the anger directly results from me being smart enough to break loose while he sits on his rear end like a good little boy. In situations of survival, I find that following rules is seldom the solution.

"Give me about five more minutes to get out of these things and I'll set you free too."

He swallows, blinks rapidly, and mumbles, "Okay."

Grabbing a handy dandy dishtowel, I wrap it around my wrist and return to the glorious stone fireplace.

Right as I'm about to blast my poor arm into the granite, a wise voice echoes in my mind. "Perhaps alchemy, Mizithra."

Yeesh! I can't believe I was about to risk breaking my arm when I could simply gather my focus and use the wonderful technique Silas taught me for getting out of handcuffs!

Taking a deep breath, I sit clumsily on the sofa, resting my pretentious chair-half bracelets on either side, and place my left hand over the lock of the steel manacle around my right wrist. Handcuff locks are super basic, but I still need my mentor's guidance. Next, I access a psychic replay of the exact moment Silas shared this knowledge with me. Impatient Mitzy would love to fast forward to the good bit, but, out of respect for Silas Willoughby, I let the memory play out in its entirety and fill me with the calm and focus I need to pull off this delicate alchemy.

The deep, wise voice of Silas echoes in my mind. "The basis of all alchemical solutions is transmutation. In this situation, the position of the lock must simply be reformed."

I scrunch up my face. "That doesn't make sense."

Silas leans back and grooms his mustache. "Let me think of another example." His eyes slowly slide from side to side as I imagine him searching for relatable parables. "Ah! Imagine you are holding an ice cube in your hand."

"Okay."

"Eventually the heat from your hand melts the ice, correct?"

I exhale. "Yeah, that's heat versus cold. It's not the same thing as locked versus unlocked."

"That is where you're wrong, Mitzy. It is precisely the same. Place your hand over the lock and visualize ice melting. And remember, your lack of belief directly affects your efficacy." He places my hand over the lock, and his milky-blue eyes stare deeply into my disbelieving grey ones. "You can feel the lock. You can feel metal binding against metal. Now begin to soften that metal, feel the metal give way. Feel the lock slipping, feel it release."

The shock of the handcuff dropping into my lap in present time jolts me out of the reverie. I was completely under Silas's spell. I relived everything he described, and then the handcuffs came off —again!

One down. One to go.

Giving my free right arm a good stretch and circle, I take another deep breath and prepare to handle the manacle on my left wrist.

Focus. Visualize. Free!

As I jump off the couch, I clap my hand over my own mouth before I can shout my news. There was absolutely not enough smashing and clattering to justify my freedom. Looks like I better do a little more wood chucking before I return to the table.

Grabbing the bits of chair previously secured to my right arm, I smash them like a woman possessed against the hearth, and the wood splinters beneath my rage.

"Almost there, Lane." As I call the news back to the deputy, I search the room for anything that could serve as a field-expedient lock pick.

A basket of yarn! A knitting needle probably wouldn't do the trick, but if there's a small crochet hook—

Bingo! Yahtzee! Gripping the hook deftly in my right hand, I quickly scrape around the now open lock openings on both cuffs. Just in case Deputy Candy inspects the debris, I want to make sure my story holds water. Now to free my temporary roommate.

The rambunctious activity surrounding my chair bashing clears my head a great deal. When I return to the kitchen, an extrasensory perception picks up on a quick flash of fear as I approach Lane. "Hey, don't worry. I picked the locks on my cuffs after I smashed that chair apart. I'll have you out of there in no time. And I'm sure there's a bathroom right upstairs. I didn't see one on the main level."

"Yeah. I'm sure you're right."

Scraping his chair back from the table to give me room to work, I set about picking the locks on his cuffs.

"I never knew you were such a reprobate, Moon."

"I get that a lot. Growing up in foster care, you can either be a victim or a survivor. I might've picked up some unattractive and possibly illegal habits, but I lived to tell the tale."

It's unclear whether his lack of a response is due to his shock and awe or his internal justice meter calculating how many years I should be serving for my possible crimes. "And you're welcome."

Lane rubs his wrists and stands quickly. "Yeah. Thanks. I guess I'm just preoccupied with trying to figure out our next move."

"Have no fear, Deputy. My plan is to grab the remaining bits of chair and smash them through a window!" Hurrying back to the living room, I grab a sturdy oak chair leg and wind up.

"Hey, wait!"

The shout from behind flusters me, and my efforts result in a swing and a miss. "Why? All I need to do is smash this window and we're out of here. If you're right about somebody monitoring the other end of that camera feed, what do you think is gonna happen when they see we're not in our chairs?"

"That's what I was thinking. Maybe we should grab a couple of the chairs pushed up against that sideboard and re-set ourselves. You know, like we're still in cuffs. If the kidnapper comes back, and we're not actually handcuffed, we can overpower them and get the keys."

"Look, I hear what you're saying, but I'm not gonna sit in this creepy house for a minute longer than I have to." I bring the hefty chair leg up over my left shoulder and swing with all my might. Imagine my surprise when I come to on the floor of the living room. "What happened?" I rub my forehead and feel a tender knot near my temple.

Lane is leaning toward the window and inspecting every inch. "The window didn't break. It must be made out of Lexan, not glass. That chair leg bounced right back and hit you in the head. You were only out for a few seconds."

Note to self: the windows are unbreakable. Time for Plan C.

"Well, this kidnapper thought of everything." Getting to my feet with the aid of the sofa, I stand still for a minute and wait for the cartoon birds to stop swirling around my head. "I'm going to find that restroom and splash some cold water on my face."

Lane nods and heads back into the kitchen. "I'll check the place for any signs of food and see if I can whip something up for us."

"Copy that."

He stops and glances over his shoulder. "Why do you say that?"

"Oh, it's a long story. Here are the highlights. It's just something that production assistants say on film sets. I picked it up on the job and decided I liked it enough to keep it around." I head upstairs with the aid of the handrail, and the sound of cupboards opening and closing indicates Lane is keeping up his end of the deal in the kitchen.

There's no mirror in the spartan bathroom. At first it seems like a minor inconvenience, but then an icy chill races across my shoulders and the hairs on the back of my neck tingle. Mirrors can be cracked. Shards could probably cut Lexan. This kidnapping wasn't planned in a day. Whoever set this up knew enough about me to know that I would try to escape, and they cleverly stymied all the usual options.

Once again the trail is unfortunately leading back to Ben. He knows me a little too well.

As I reach the bottom of the stairs, I sigh and make a beeline for my water. "Did you find anything?"

Lane smiles weakly. "Some white bread that didn't have any mold on it, some bologna, and sliced cheese. No condiments. Is that okay?"

"Are you kidding? That sounds like a feast fit for a king. Sign me up."

CHAPTER 8
ERICK

THERE'S A MOUNTAIN of paperwork that I need to get squared away, but my mind only has one track this morning. Mitzy's "friend" Shady Ben should be on a plane home by now. It shouldn't bother me that she hasn't called or texted. I trust her. We trust each other. That's what all good relationships are built on, or so I'm told.

Work, or the grunt work in the Army, has always served as a great distraction in the past. Let's see what's cooking on the Pin Cherry blotter. Pushing back from my vintage desk, I run my hands over the dent in the left-hand drawer and smile. A lot of great sheriffs sat in this chair before me. The deputies always poke fun and tell me I'm a cheapskate because I won't spring for a new chair or desk. I generally tell them that I think the taxpayers' dollars are better spent keeping the community safe, but the real reason is I can't bear to part with these pieces of history.

Sure, there's a weird spring that pokes me just under the left shoulder blade, but that serves to remind me of the time Sheriff Hansen's wife came in and fired her pea shooter into his empty chair after she found out he was stepping out on her. Honestly, he's one of the few less-than-stellar folks who held this position. For the most part, they've all been solid, upstanding people who had their lives pretty locked down. They each sat at this desk and laid the foundation for the job I'm doing today.

Mitzy can take care of herself. She's proven that more than once. I suppose this nagging feeling in the back of my head is nothing more than good, old-fashioned jealousy. It's been so long since I experienced the emotion my brain's having a little trouble identifying it.

Time to get to work.

Sauntering into the bullpen, I take a quick head count. "Paulsen, looks like we're one short?"

My best deputy and right hand around the station, Deputy Paulsen, gets to her feet and widens her stance. She's got a low center of gravity and enough body mass to take down a perp twice her size. She's a good linebacker to have on your team.

"You betcha, Sheriff. I ran the roll call this

morning and Deputy Candy was nowhere to be seen. When I got back to my desk, here, there was an email from him saying he had a family emergency and he'd be out for a few days. Wasn't sent through secure channels. Came from his personal email. Something musta happened after he got home last night."

"Good to know. Give him our best and make sure he uses the appropriate leave codes for his absence."

"10-4."

The weight of the silent phone in my front pocket refuses to be ignored. "I'm going to run a quick patrol over by the library construction site. Silas Willoughby reported a couple of undesirables running around the site as he headed home last night."

"10-4, Sheriff. We'll have dispatch reach out if anything comes up."

She drops back into her seat and shuffles some reports on her desk, but the unspoken name on her lips hangs in the air, clear as day. Thank the stars she's too professional to ask.

After running a quick safety check on my vehicle, I slide into the passenger seat, turn the key, and the engine roars to life. She's not as nimble as my Nova, but she's got power. Bit of a sleeper, Deputy Johnson always says. I made adjustments to the tuning and squeezed a few more horsepower out of her eight cylinders, just in case. Not a lot of high-speed chases around the harbor, but I'm not looking to be caught with my pants down if there are.

I almost always patrol with my windows down —except in the dead of winter. It's as easy to hear trouble, as it is to see it. The refreshing breeze rolling across the lake brings news of an early fall. Fine by me. The humidity and the pesky flying critters have taken it out of me this summer.

On the upside, I'll be happy to fill my role as head judge of the baking contest and ease into cooler weather and the gorgeous fall color that will soon embrace the entire area.

Boy, that phone isn't playing fair.

Sliding it out of my pocket, I convince myself I have an urgent need to check the time. Turns out it's less than five minutes from when I left the station. The last time I had this feeling in my gut, Mitzy was working as a confidential informant for the force and got grabbed by a couple of criminals outside Final Destination.

Adjusting my grip on the steering wheel, I look up as the quaint old watering hole looms into view. Couldn't hurt to stop in and have a little chat with Lars. Most days he gets more gossip than the quilting circle.

As I open the door of my patrol car, my cell

pings. I nearly drop the thing in my haste to read the message.

It's from Mitzy. Relief trickles down my spine.

"Taking a road trip. Ben wants more sightseeing. I'll keep you posted."

The relief vanishes, and the unease seeps into its place. Some details or an actual phone call would be nice. Maybe Lars can take my mind off my troubles.

The well-worn door opens with a welcoming creak, and I pause inside as my eyes adjust to the dim interior. This place has one mission, serve strong drinks at a great price. Lars accomplishes his honorable goal by keeping overhead low. You won't find any frills here.

"Happy hour starts at 4:30."

"Morning, Lars. How's the fishin' been?"

"Sheriff! Haven't seen you in a month of Sundays—I'm happy to say." He slaps his large hand on the bar and chuckles. "I'm awful glad my patrons have been keeping their noses clean. If their stories are to be believed, the fish are twice as big as they were last year and three times as eager to jump on a hook. You pull an elk tag this year?"

"I did, but I don't think I'll be able to use it. My mom's eyesight has gotten quite a bit worse, and I'm not sure I'd feel comfortable leaving her alone for a four-day trek up north. Although, her sister keeps threatening to come for a visit. If that happens I might be able to swing it. So I'm hanging onto it for now, but if you know someone who's looking, I still have time to name my second."

"Sure enough. I'll keep it in mind, Sheriff. By the by, if you're looking for *Daisy*, you missed her by several hours."

The name catches me off guard for a split second, and then all the memories of Mitzy's undercover barmaid operation and that sexy red wig come rushing back. I join him in a hearty laugh and shake my head. "Just checkin' on the latest news about town, not for anyone in particular."

Lars hauls a huge plastic tub of bar mix out from under the bar and uses the bowls as handy scoops. "Sure. You betcha. Not much to tell. She showed up last night with that scrappy dark-haired sidekick from Arizona. They ran up quite a bar tab, which Mitzy paid, and she tossed me her keys before she left. Said they were gonna walk home."

The strange feeling in the back of my head rockets to the front. "Do you still have the keys?"

"Sure thing." Lars punches a button on the register, the cash drawer pops open, and he fishes out Mitzy's key ring. "You want me to hang onto it, or you wanna take care of her car yourself."

My answer gets waylaid by my swirling worries.

I used to get feelings like this right before artillery fire started ripping through the night sky in Afghanistan. I wish there was a better name for it than women's intuition, but, whatever it is, my gut is squirrelly with it. "That's the thing, Lars. Her Jeep isn't out there."

Lars drops the keys on the bar and rubs his chin. "Come to think of it, the parking lot was empty when I got here today. She probably came back to get it early and used a backup set. You know, since the place was locked up."

My head goes into overdrive, trying to convince my gut that this could be true. "Possibly. She did text me that her and Ben were taking a road trip. Apparently he was so impressed with the area, he wanted to see more before he headed back to Arizona. She said she'd keep me posted." My left hand reaches into my pocket and squeezes my phone. "I'm sure she has more than one set of keys. You're probably right about that."

The bar owner picks up the keys and tosses them straight up in the air, catching them in the same hand rhythmically. "I suppose, but last night she was acting like she couldn't get that guy out of town fast enough. They had a bit of a tiff over some money she supposedly owed him, from back in the day, and she promised to pay him back with interest, and buy him a first-class ticket this morning.

Didn't seem like the kind of disagreement that would lead to a road trip."

My head jumps in with all cylinders firing. "You know women. Impulsive, unpredictable, never can tell what they'll do."

Lars tosses the keys toward me, and I catch them in my right hand.

"I think my ex-wife would disagree with you, Sheriff. She always said I was the impulsive one. I bought this place without even looking at the books. Something about it just felt right, you know?"

I knew what he was talking about, and I also knew when something just felt wrong. Mitzy and this road-trip story felt wrong. "Sure do. I better get going, Lars. You let me know if you hear anything interesting."

He kindly avoided saying her name, only chuckled for a minute, and replied, "You got it, Sheriff."

I walk the perimeter of Final Destination to make sure Mitzy's Jeep isn't tucked behind the dumpster or something.

No sign of it.

Maybe she did take a road trip. It wasn't beyond the scope of possibilities for her to do something impulsive. Honestly, it seems like just about everything she does is spur of the moment. I don't know what power this Shady Ben holds over her, but I suppose we all have exes.

The rest of my patrol through Pin Cherry is uneventful. Great for the community at large, but terrible at taking my mind off imagined concerns.

Maybe I'll grab an early lunch at the diner and see if Odell has anything to share.

The cozy diner is bursting with welcome tourists who come up to enjoy the plethora of pies that will be available at the baking competition. A couple years back a national news outlet picked up the story of the winner's pie, and things sort of snowballed from there.

I take a seat at the counter, and Tally stops with a pot of coffee in one hand and an empty mug in the other. "What's it going to be, Sheriff? You need more coffee, or are you in an iced tea kind of mood?"

"You know, I think an iced tea with a nice thick wedge of lemon is just what the doctor ordered."

She shuffles off to fill my request, and Odell gives me a nod from the kitchen. It's hard to imagine why a man with such a big heart and honest soul never remarried after things went south with Mitzy's grandmother, Myrtle Isadora. I only have an outsider's perspective, but I would've thought by the time that woman hit her third or fourth husband Odell mighta felt free to pick a new bride of his own. But I suppose there's something romantic about their story. They did rekindle their deep friendship at the end of Isadora's life. I should specify the end of her earthly life.

My head still spins every time I think about ghosts being real. I would've called it a trick of the imagination, or maybe even just the mind's desire to believe in such a thing, but I've felt Isadora's ghost pass through me, and I've seen her move things around Mitzy's apartment.

That's the kind of first-hand evidence a lawman can't argue with. Course, it's also not the kind of thing a lawman is going to run around telling the world about, so their secret is safe with me.

Odell walks out with a cheeseburger and fries. The mere sight of those golden pieces of potato makes my heart ache. Mitzy loves french fries.

Get a grip, Harper! She went on a little road trip with an old friend. Cool your jets.

"How's it looking out there, Sheriff?"

"Not as good as that burger, Johnson."

Odell chuckles. "Just remember how good this burger tastes when you're judging that pie contest this weekend."

His comment catches me off guard, and I stop with a fistful of fries halfway to my mouth. "Johnson, you're not suggesting this is a bribe?"

"Not me, Sheriff. Just pointing out the refinement of flavors I've put together for you here."

Shaking my head and smiling, I straighten my shoulders and salute the man who served decades before me, but still outranks me.

He returns the gesture and meanders back to his grill.

He didn't ask about Mitzy, and he didn't offer any information. Likely as anything, that means he hasn't seen her. He may be a man of few words, but he's got a soft spot in his heart for that girl, and if he had any news, he would at least share it with me.

For a few minutes my troubles are forgotten, as I lose myself in the delicious lunch. Savoring one of the crisp pickle chips brings half a smile to my face. All good things must come to an end.

I take the last swig of iced tea, leave a few bills on the counter, and wave as I head back to the cruiser.

Maybe I'll drive past the bookshop one more time.

As I make the left turn from Main Street onto First Avenue, the "Closed" sign is the first thing that catches my eye. Now, the bookstore being closed when Twiggy is out of town isn't a huge shock, but all the lights are off. You can usually see that ostentatious chandelier from two blocks away when it's fired up.

There's no Jeep parked in the alley, either.

My cruise around town has given me nothing but more questions. I should give it a few more hours before I swing past the airport, flash my badge, and see if a Benicio Alvarez boarded any southbound flights today.

Yeah, that seems like a perfectly normal thing to do.

CHAPTER 9

HEY, UNIVERSE, waking up in a puddle of drool better not be the new normal. The good news is that this time I'm on a slightly comfortable couch, and not handcuffed to a wooden chair.

The bad news is that my head feels as thick as the sludge at the bottom of a commercial espresso machine. And, as a former mediocre barista, I can assure you that you don't ever want to see what I'm talking about.

Sitting up, I wipe my mouth with the back of my hand and rake my fingers through my wild hair.

"Candy? I mean, Lane, did you find a way out of this place yet?"

Silence.

The lack of response forces me to my feet, and I

support my head with one hand as I shuffle toward the kitchen.

Empty.

Before I head upstairs to search the remaining rooms, I turn on the tap and shove my head under the faucet. Some of the water goes in my mouth, some of the water runs over my flushed face—it's one of the best things that has happened since last night.

Swiping at the water, I trundle upstairs and check the bedrooms.

When I open the door to the second bedroom, Deputy Candy jumps in surprise. "You scared me."

The bologna sandwich doesn't seem to be agreeing with me, and I have no patience for this guy's nonsense. "I scared you? Some anonymous crazy person kidnapped us, you're the actual, trained deputy, and I scared *you*. Boy, this doesn't bode well for our survival."

He fusses with his pillow like an overpaid maid, and finally swings his feet onto the floor. "I must've been super tired. I fell right asleep after lunch."

"Lunch!" A forced sardonic laughter erupts from my throat. "That's rich. The last time I called a bologna sandwich lunch was when I lived with foster family number five. After that I got lunch money by whatever means necessary and upgraded myself to meatloaf surprise and canned pudding."

Yawning loudly, I rub the sleep from the corners of my eyes. "We need a plan to get out of here. I don't know if you've given it any thought, but the fact that both of us fell asleep immediately after we ate our sandwiches seems like a good indication that the food is drugged. So unless you want to keep feasting on tainted morsels, and losing chunks of time to heaven only knows what, I suggest you put that genius brain of yours to work figuring a way out of this mess."

The mask of irritation that pinches his features is getting on my nerves. I didn't plan on running a dictatorship, but if he's not gonna pull his weight, what are my options? Wandering toward the window, I glance down at the surroundings. "I don't see any dwellings nearby, but your patrol car is parked in the driveway. So, if we can get out of this perfect mousetrap, we'll at least have a ride back to civilization."

He feels his front pockets and his shirt pockets. "I don't have the keys."

"Keys!" This time my laughter is genuine. "This guy and his keys. I don't need keys, Deputy. You get me out of this house, and I can start the car."

His face strains with concern.

"Don't worry yourself, Lane. I'd never use my skills for evil. I'm on your side of the law now."

Whatever they put in the food is wreaking

havoc on my extra senses, but for a moment I swear I feel a wave of regret roll off the man-child. "Did you have any ideas you wanted to throw in the hat?"

He shakes his head. "Seems like you're better with this sort of thing than I am."

I throw my hands in the air. "Seems like it! Here's what we're going to do. We'll methodically check every window in this house. I suppose if they have replaced one window with some type of bulletproof glass, they all are, but I'm checking all the same. Then I'm going to search every drawer in this house for a hairpin or paperclip, anything smaller than a crochet hook, and see if I can pick the lock on the front door. If none of those things are successful, I'm going to throw myself on the floor and pitch the biggest hissy fit this side of the equator!" Without waiting for his reply or protest, I march downstairs to retrieve my trusty oak chair leg.

Learning from my mistakes, I angle my head out of harm's way as I proceed to take a swing at each window of the small two-story farmhouse.

I could take you through the adventure window by window, but I'd warrant a guess that you'd get tired of hearing "it bounced off, without so much as cracking the Lexan."

Repeat for each and every one of the eighteen windows.

Now that my failure is complete, I can proceed to the drawer-searching part of my plan.

The kitchen contains basic silverware, a meager set of utensils, and, most importantly—no knives.

There are no additional drawers on the first floor, but the second floor has a small desk in one room, which yields three paperclips, and I discover a lone bobby pin at the back of a drawer in the bathroom.

Armed with my pathetic set of options, I march toward the front door with a confidence I don't possess.

This won't be the first lock I've picked without an official lock-pick kit, but it is the first deadbolt.

Unsurprisingly, Lane doesn't lift a finger to aid in the execution of my stellar, multi-step escape plan. No problem. I'm used to pulling myself up by my bootstraps. If I'd paid closer attention to Silas's training, or maybe if the sedatives weren't messing with my head, I could use alchemy to open the front door. Currently, that's not an option. A simple handcuff lock is a far cry from a deadbolt.

Sliding the extra paperclip and the bobby pin onto the hem of my short-sleeved tee, I proceed to bend the remaining two clips into makeshift tools. Paperclip number one simply gets opened to a forty-five degree angle, while paperclip number two is straightened out completely, and then bent directly in half, squeezing the two pieces tightly.

Inserting the compressed loop end into the lock about a quarter of an inch, I carefully bend the long end parallel to the door. This piece now becomes my tension wrench. Using the right angle clip to test the pins in the barrel, I discover a grand total of seven. That's not good news.

Well, no sense getting discouraged before I even start.

Taking a deep breath, I insert the tension wrench, apply solid pressure, and carefully pick at each pin. The first three push up to the shearline with ease, and then things go south.

Frustration sets in, and I attempt to use a steady raking motion to raise the rest of the pins, but that's when I realize what I'm up against.

"There's a second cylinder directly above the first!"

Angrily tossing my paperclip tools to the floor by the threshold, I pound my fist against the door and scream. "Aargh!" I know no one can hear me, but sometimes inanimate objects just need to be told what's what.

A strange tingle lifts a few hairs on the back of my neck, but as I turn, hoping to push through my brain fog and tune in, Deputy Candy's thunderous descent of the staircase steals my attention.

"Mitzy? Are you okay? Did I hear you scream?" His heart is racing more than I would expect from simply running down the stairs, but if he's suffering the aftereffects of whatever sedative was in our food, I suppose that makes sense.

"I'm fine. Just had a minor disagreement with the door, that's all."

His tight shoulders soften and he exhales loudly. "Oh, that's all. I thought something serious happened."

Hunger, the side effects of unknown toxins, and overall irritation with the deputy's lack of cooperation have gotten the better of me. "Yeah, something more serious did happen! I thought I had a real shot at picking this lock and getting the heck out of this nuthouse, but it's impossible. I mean, not impossible for a pro. But it's absolutely impossible without a proper set of tools, and even then it could take hours."

"Hey, I'm sorry it didn't work out. Seems like you know what you're talking about. I'm glad you gave it a try. I wish we had a lock pick set, but I'm sure Ben thought of that, you know. He'd know you'd try this, right?"

Once again, his insistence that Ben is the one who put us here has some merit. Beni is loosely familiar with my history, and if he had left any decent tools, or a sharp knife, I might've been able to get somewhere with even a double-barreled lock like this one. "Do you really think it was Ben? I've known him for years, and he never really seemed like the kidnapper type."

Candy motions toward the living room. "Would you mind if we sit down while we talk? My head really is pounding."

"Sure. My work here is done." I sulk along behind him and sink onto the sofa, keeping my distance. We may be co-captives, but he still gives me the creeps. "So I was asking you what made you so sure Ben did this." I gesture for him to pick up the discussion where we left off.

"First of all, there were only three of us on the road. The last thing I remember is picking the two of you up. Then I woke here. I suppose if you're determined to look at any *possible* options . . . It is *possible* that some unknown person shot me with a hypodermic needle through the open and moving window of my cruiser, and then managed to get into and stop the vehicle right as I lost consciousness, but before I totally lost control of the car, then bring the whole vehicle to a halt. And finally, drive us out here."

I open my mouth to protest, but he rudely puts up a hand.

"Wait, I forgot about the part where this anonymous assailant then disposes of Ben—I can only assume to silence him permanently—and locks up the two of us in this remote house. Reason being, either this mystery kidnapper was after you or me, or, if we're really throwing around crazy ideas, maybe both of us. I suppose that is *possible*."

"Fine. I get your point. You don't have to look so obnoxiously smug." Crossing my arms, I lean back into the sofa and default into a solid pout.

"Mitzy, I have no idea what this person's endgame is or how long we may be trapped. Would you consider calling a truce?"

Letting my arms fall heavily into my lap, I nod. "On one condition."

"Name it."

"Get on board with this idea of escaping. You flew through high school and college, and aced pretty much every written exam at the academy, if rumors can be believed, so there has to be some solution buried somewhere inside that head of yours. If you want a truce, I want three ideas by dinner."

A warm smile melts his nervous expression. "I think that can be arranged. Why don't you make another pass through the rooms down here, and see if you can find any supplies? Something like possibly a rope, anything made out of sturdy metal, or maybe some matches. I don't have an idea yet, but my brain sort of needs to know what it's working with before it can piece together a solution. I guess I suffer from lack of imagination. More of a problem solver from a practical standpoint."

I shrug. "And what are you gonna do while I make another search of the house?"

"Honestly, I don't know what time it is, but doing something with my hands helps me stay calm. I was wondering if I could make dinner? I'm sure I can find something better than bologna sandwiches."

"It's not like I have a lot of options, Lane. I'd rather we put our heads together and get out of here before things get worse, than waste all our energy bickering. You've got yourself a deal." I extend my hand to shake on our agreement, and he blushes before he meets my grip.

His handshake isn't firm or confident. It's sort of like a dead fish, but hot and sweaty.

Trying not to yank my hand free, I end the handshake as politely as possible and resume my search.

Returning to the kitchen with the spoils of my search, a surprising aroma greets me. "Something smells *good*?"

Lane looks up from the stove and grins. "Grilled cheese and tomato soup. I know it's not really a summer dish, but it beats cold, processed meat."

"Sounds good to me. Would you like to know what I discovered?"

He dishes out the soup, cuts the grilled sandwiches from corner to corner and heads toward the table. "Of course. You can fill me in over dinner."

Doesn't he mean over kidnap rations?

Lane arranges two places opposite each other and retrieves an unbroken chair from the corner to replace the one I demolished earlier.

I dump my haul on the end of the table near my steaming bowl of tomato soup. Before I launch into my tale, I dip the corner of my gooey cheese sandwich into the soup and take a huge, dripping bite. "Hey, it's not bad. Where did you find the soup?"

He blushes and looks down at the table. "It's ketchup, milk, salt and pepper. I was working with what I had."

"Well, if I were a judge on the 'Cook Your Way Out of Kidnapping' reality TV show, I'd give you top marks."

He looks up with an uncomfortable amount of admiration filling his eyes and whispers, "Thanks, Mitzy."

Yikes! Creep factor returns. Powering through a few more dunked bites of sandwich, I take a breather to reveal my loot. "Here's what I found." I line each item up as I call it out.

"Nail clippers. No rope, but a fist-size ball of twine and two small balls of yarn. Mini sewing kit with thread, buttons, and a safety pin. Bottle of castor oil. Box of frighteningly old matches, with five wooden matches remaining. First place ribbon for debate."

At the sight of the ribbon, Lane chokes on his grilled cheese and pats his chest as he guzzles some water.

"You all right?"

He nods his head. "Yeah. Shouldn't talk with my mouth full. I was wondering what you thought we could do with a ribbon?"

"Oh, nothing. I was thinking it might give us a clue about the person who trapped us here."

"Yeah, good idea." He takes another long sip of water and clears his throat once. "Okay, I'll get busy on solutions. If all goes well, we'll be out of here by morning." His words are encouraging, but my psychic feelers sense regret. "Sounds good. Thanks again for throwing together this delicious dinner."

He smiles too easily, and my discomfort ratchets up.

CHAPTER 10
ERICK

"Hey, Mom, I'm home."

The indomitable Gracie Harper steps out of the kitchen grinning from ear to ear. "Ricky! How was your day, honey?"

"Not great, Mom."

"Oh goodness. Did one of those nasty criminals get away?"

"No, Ma. Nothing that bad. Just a little mix up with Mitzy, you know?"

She nods, and her caring smile makes all the teasing at work worthwhile. Not everyone understands why a man my age would share a home with his mother. I bought the house for her after I got out of the Army, but I hadn't planned to live with her. When the problems with her eyesight began, there wasn't much we could do to prevent macular degeneration from taking its course. I broke the lease on my apartment and moved into the house I thought was to be hers.

The deputies love to call me an "old maid" down at the station, always giving me a hard time about my mommy packing my lunch or pinning notes to my shirt. Neither of those things ever happens, but playful teasing is all part of the camaraderie, and I gave up fighting it a long time ago.

The truth is, my mom is an amazingly strong woman who worked two or three jobs so she could afford to raise me on her own and send me to college. Buying her a house hardly seems a fitting repayment, but it's a start.

We have a system that keeps us squared away. I run all the errands, get the groceries, and read her favorite books to her if we can't find them on tape, or CD if she's desperate. I keep asking her if she'd like some kind of MP3 player so she can take advantage of the new downloadable audiobooks, but she says she's too old to bother with new technology.

For her part, she does the laundry, and makes most of the meals. I hired someone to come in once a week and tidy up, because, obviously, it's not that easy to clean if you can't clearly see your surroundings.

The system works. We're both pretty happy.

The only major drawback has been a bit of a crimp in my dating life.

Of course, until I met Mitzy Moon, that really wasn't much of an issue either.

A warmth spreads across my chest.

I got lucky with Mitzy, though. Not *that* kind of lucky, the kinda lucky where you meet that once-in-a-lifetime girl and she totally understands why you live with your mother—because she lives with a ghost.

What are the odds?

"Ricky?"

"Yeah, Ma. I'm gonna go take a hot shower and then I'll dish up supper. Sound good?"

"That sounds great, honey. I'll listen to one of my 'Cat Who' tapes until you're ready."

Helping my mom to the sofa, I kiss the top of her head as she reaches toward her well-used tape player.

A lengthy hot shower is a rare treat. In the Army there was never time for lengthy showers, and the water was never what I would call hot. Now, with my 24/7 on-call sheriff duties, I squeeze in a quick shower whenever I can get one.

I wish I could say this luxury is relaxing, but I can't get rid of the unsettling heaviness in my gut, and I can't get Mitzy Moon out of my mind. Although, that's not all bad.

Basketball shorts, a worn out T-shirt, and bare feet are the perfect wardrobe for my unhappy night in.

"How hungry are you, Mom?"

"I'm pretty hungry tonight, dear. You can give me an extra scoop of vegetables."

"10-4." I slice a thick portion of juicy meatloaf for myself, and a smaller slice for my mom. Her scalloped potatoes are one of my favorite side dishes, and she knows how much I love steamed broccoli. Careful to leave a little broccoli for my lunch tomorrow, I divide the remaining between the two of us. "Supper is served."

She clicks her tape player off and joins me at our small round kitchen table. When I was a boy, it seemed like an enormous table, and the light-blue material covering the chairs could have been leather for all I knew. But everything seemed big in our tiny one-bedroom apartment. Maybe I'll buy her some new furniture for Christmas. Seems overly indulgent, since she can't see it, but I figure she'll appreciate the gesture. Plus, my bare legs squeak against the vinyl covering these ancient chairs.

"So, Ricky, tell me what's got you down in the dumps."

"It's nothing, Ma. Boring relationship stuff."

"Now, Ricky, I'm your mother. Nothing about your life bores me. I may not have all the answers, and I sure as sugar can't see to save my life, but my ears still work. So you tell me what's bothering you. It'll help to get it off your chest."

"Okay, Ma." I give her a condensed version of the Mitzy and Shady Ben story, and read her the two texts. A second one came in after lunch.

"Doesn't sound like Mitzy, dear."

"What do you mean? She's the most impulsive and unpredictable person I know. What about this latest snafu doesn't sound like her?"

"Oh, not that. I meant the texts. You know, maybe because your eyes work, you don't listen so good. The wording of those texts just doesn't sound like some of the other stuff you've read me from her."

As soon as she says it, that heavy weight in my gut sinks even lower. "I think something's wrong, Ma. I don't mean in our relationship. I think something's happened to her."

My mother sets down her fork and knife and nods. "What have I always told you, Ricky? You follow your instincts. They'll never steer you wrong."

"Okay, Ma. As soon as I finish supper and clear the table, I'll head over to the bookshop and see what I can find."

"That's my boy."

The rest of supper's conversation is occupied

with stories of who's entering the baking contest, and what gifts have been sent her way, hoping to influence her son. She tells the stories as though the attempted bribery infuriates her, but the huge grin on her face and the pride in her voice says otherwise.

She heads back to the sofa, and I clear up before hopping into my civvies.

Outside, I reach for the door of my cruiser and I'm greeted with a wildcat's feral growl.

Jumping back, it takes a minute to catch my breath and talk some sense into myself. I crouch, grab my penlight, and peer under the car. Two large golden eyes reflect the light back at me. "Pyewacket? Is that you?" Here's hoping.

He slithers out from under the vehicle, steps toward me, and without thinking I hold out my hand.

The terrifying beast drops a piece of fabric in my hand.

Shining the light on it, I see no identifying marks. But Mitzy has taught me well. Pyewacket never does anything superfluous. I slip the fabric in my front pocket and open the patrol car. "Can I offer you a ride home, Pye?"

With unnerving human reaction, he nods his broad head, hops in the vehicle, and curls up in the passenger seat.

Mitzy was right about this guy. He actually seems to understand English.

At the bookshop, I pull down the alley and approach the side door.

If anyone sees me right now, I'll— No time for what ifs. Mitzy says ghosts are real.

Pressing the bell, the satisfying tones resound inside the building.

Without Mitzy's ghost gift, I'm forced to possibly make a complete fool of myself. I lean against the door and call out, "Isadora? Isadora, if you're in there, I really need you to open this door. I think something happened to—"

The handle twists, and my blood runs cold as I step away from the sorcery.

Swallowing hard, I grip the handle and drag the door open.

Pyewacket races in without hesitation, and I lean my head around the door. "Can I come in?"

Reaching my hand in to feel for a light switch, I encounter a cold swath of air and goosebumps pepper my forearm. "I wish I could see you, Isadora. But based on experience, I'd say these goosebumps mean you're here. I'm coming in."

Closing the door behind me, I feel my hand along the wall until it bumps the light switch. As soon as the light floods the hall, I see the keypad for the alarm and a whole new series of concerns wash over me.

"Blast! If that alarm goes off and one of the deputies finds me in here— I have no cover story. Isadora, any chance you know the alarm code?"

A prickly coldness seems to grip my hand and slide off in the direction of the back room.

Pyewacket meows and leads the way toward the desk. The chilly touch once again draws my hand toward a pen. "Oh, right. Pen and paper. Hold on."

Grabbing a piece of paper and a pen, I set the items on the table and step back. No matter how many times I've told myself that Isadora's ghost really lives in the bookshop, the sight of the pen moving of its own free will, scrawling out numbers on a sheet of paper, is terrifying.

Just as she finishes the sequence, the final warning beeps start with the alarm system. I grab the sheet of paper, race to the keypad, and type in the eight-digit code.

"It worked! You're a lifesaver, Isadora."

The coolness seems to have vanished from the hall, and Pyewacket is calling out from the bottom of the stairs. This has to be the strangest investigation I've ever been on.

Obediently, I follow the cat upstairs. When I reach the delicate brass candle sconce, I hesitate. "I don't want to invade Mitzy's privacy, Isadora. Are you sure it's okay for me to go into the apartment without permission?"

The chill passes straight through me and even pushes me forward. A sensation, which creates a brief nausea in my gut. "I'm calling that a yes."

I tilt the handle down, and the bookcase door slides open. Inside, the lights ramp up automatically and illuminate Mitzy's infamous murder wall.

On the rolling corkboard, in ghost scrawls, Isadora has lost no time. She has a card for Mitzy, a card for Shady Ben—I'm pleased she's referred to him by his proper name—and a card for Deputy Candy. "Why is there a card for my deputy, Isadora?"

The card on the board twists left and right beneath its tack, and Pyewacket smacks my right thigh with his shockingly powerful paw.

"Hey, take it easy on me. I'm new to this, guys. Give me a second to put it all together." I don't know how Mitzy does this! She just talks to ghosts and takes clues from cats and solves murders that stump my entire department. And then—

"The fabric!"

Pyewacket meows loudly.

I can almost swear it's some version of "I told you so."

Now I really am losing my mind. Removing the chunk of fabric from my pocket, I examine the fabric carefully. "Looks like a piece from the hem of a pair of pants, clearly removed by a clever feline. Is it a uniform?"

Pyewacket's vocalization seems to cheer me on.

My eyes light up. "This is a piece of Deputy Candy's uniform. And he's the one who responded to that alarm code yesterday morning. But he sent an email last night about a family emergency —hold on."

Slipping out my phone, I call dispatch. "It's Sheriff Harper. Can you check the logs and tell me what time Deputy Candy called in the alarm code at the Bell, Book & Candle?" There's a pause while she searches. "You sure? Just a call from the security company? Thanks."

A chill touches my shoulder, and Pye sits eagerly at my feet.

"Bad news, guys. That alarm code never went through dispatch. The only way Candy would've known the alarm sounded here at the bookshop is if he had hacked into the system somehow and redirected the alerts to his cell phone, rather than dispatch. Sounds like something he might've learned in that blasted surveillance class I sent him to! I'm thinking Shady Ben might not be to blame."

Pyewacket rubs affectionately against my leg, and I take that as a good sign.

"Isadora, did Mitzy say anything to you about

taking a road trip?" Listen to me! Now I'm talking to ghosts.

A sharpie lifts off a stack of 3 x 5 cards on the coffee table, and the message reveals itself. "She said airport."

"That's what I thought! Does this same code work to open the garage?"

Pyewacket growls with excitement and darts out of the apartment.

Without waiting for Isadora to scratch out a reply, I blindly follow the caracal down the wrought-iron staircase and into the alley.

Tapping the code into the keypad results in the satisfying grind of a motor, but when the garage door gets a few feet off the ground, the sight of Mitzy's Jeep replaces the satisfaction with horror.

Nobody heads out on a road trip without their vehicle.

She's been taken!

CHAPTER 11

SEVERAL HOURS LATER, when my eyelids lazily drift open, I'm surprised by the darkness in the living room. Either Deputy Candy is reducing the amount of sedative he's putting in my food, or I'm building up a tolerance.

Yes, I figured out he was drugging the food early on, but until I could figure out why, I felt it was best to keep that under my hat. It doesn't seem like he's been drugging his own food, so right out of the gate it's my plan to continue fake sleeping and see if he's up to any shenanigans while he thinks I'm out cold.

Reaching out with all of my psychic senses, I receive a nasty reward.

"What are you doing in my house, you sly cookie?"

A ghost! An angry June Cleaver starring in *Leave it to Beaver* ghost!

The old "answer a question with a question" gambit seems like a solid option. "Quick question. Am I the only one awake right now?"

"If you're inquiring about my sweet great-grandson, he's sleeping like an angel in the other room. He's straightened everything up for you, but I'm afraid things look like a bum rap for your friend."

"Which friend?"

She places her petite fists on her narrow hips, and her perfect A-line skirt sways as she shakes her head.

Before she answers, I know she means Beni. "Where is he? Is he locked in the basement?"

"It's not my place to say." She straightens her thin belt.

Great, Miss Manners is going to be uncooperative. "So this was your house?"

"It still is my house, you silly girl. What are those infernal slacks you're wearing? In my day, women did not wear trousers."

Oh brother. "Well, I'm afraid it's sixty or seventy years past your day, and jeans are all the rage. Why are you trapped here?"

"Trapped? A woman's work is never done. I

tidy up, I make sure the pillowcases are pressed, and the floors vacuumed every day."

"And your husband?"

Her perfect expression turns dangerous, and beneath that innocent set of pearls lurks a terrible tale.

Probably best to get straight to the point with this ghost of etiquette past. "I hate to be the one to tell you this, but you died. I don't know when, or how, but—"

"Oh, I can tell you how, Miss Smarty Pants. My husband locked me in this house, kept me a prisoner, even from my own mother. I'll tell you what! I went stark raving mad. I did. I tried everything to convince him to let me go to church, at least, but he wouldn't hear of it. So on Easter morning 1959, I put on my best Easter dress and my pearls. I vacuumed the entire house and made the bed."

A terrible premonition hits, and the end of her story reveals itself to me in a series of images I don't want to share. The dutiful homemaker seems to have hung herself in the basement. "I'm so sorry for what happened to you. Why are you still trapped here?"

"A woman's work is never done." Tears leak from the corners of her eyes as she repeats the mantra that has no doubt been her safeguard for these many decades.

"What's your name?"

"Phyllis. Phyllis Anderson."

"I'm sorry for the terrible things you must've endured, Phyllis. And I'm sorry your husband pushed you to take your own life—"

Her soft, round features turn harsh and angular. "Take my own life! What kind of gobbledygook are you talking? That's a filthy lie. Until someone finds out what he really did, I'll never leave! I'm not saying it never crossed my mind. It broke my heart when I thought about all the bridge games I was missing, social invitations, the fashion . . ." Her eyes drift off to memories. "I used to get a brand-new Easter dress and a brand-new Christmas dress every year. Once he locked me away, I had to wear the same thing, over and over."

I'm sure Grams would adore chatting fashion with this woman, but I have bigger fish to fry. "Phyllis, are you saying your husband killed you?"

"Cross my heart and hope to die. He strangled me, right up there in our bedroom, because I refused to make him breakfast unless he would take me to church. I just got so tired of it all. I thought if I put my foot down—"

She's weeping huge ghost tears now, and I know from experience with Grams I'm powerless to provide her with a handkerchief. "He strangled you, and then he hung you in the basement to make it look like a suicide? With the forensics available in the 1950s, I'm not surprised he got away with it. But what about the funeral? Didn't people ask questions?"

"I shouldn't wonder that no one cared. He made up quite a lot of lies over the years to cover my absence from church and our friend's parties. I suppose he had them all convinced that I belonged in a sanitarium. They probably thought he was the generous one, taking care of his insane wife. It wasn't fair."

"It absolutely isn't fair, but if you've been watching us over the last few days, I think you've seen that your great-grandson is about to do the same thing to me."

One hand flies up to cover her tiny strawberry mouth, and the other clutches her pearls. "He wouldn't!"

"He already is. If you help me out of here, Phyllis, I will tell the world what really happened. I promise you, your husband will be brought to justice, posthumously, and you'll be able to cross over and finally find the peace you deserve."

"Gosh, do you think?"

"I know. Help me and I'll help you. Cross my heart and hope to die."

Phyllis swallows hard and nods. "I've heard him

talking to himself in his room. He's madly in love with you."

"It's the *madly* part that concerns me."

"Well, you aren't just whistling Dixie. He wants you to be his wife, make his meals, straighten up his house, and take care of him. He has a very old-fashioned sense about relationships."

"I hate to burst your bubble, Phyllis, but that's never going to happen. Now, are you going to help me or not?"

She puts one hand on her tiny waist and sizes me up. "We need to get you decked out in a proper outfit, and then I'll show you where he keeps the sedatives."

My ears perk up like a hunting dog. "You know where he keeps the drugs?"

"Drugs? Oh no! There are no drugs in this house. Just a mild prescription sedative."

This woman and her hairsplitting! "Unless you can magically alter clothes, there's no way we're getting me into any of your hand-me-downs."

"Oh, silly goose, we won't have to. He's stocked the closet upstairs with all sorts of lovely skirts and sweaters sets in your size."

All right. Now it's time to hit the panic button. "Fine. I'll wear a sweater set, but I want you to show me where the sedatives are first."

She drifts purposefully into the kitchen and gestures to the high cupboard above the small refrigerator. "It's in there. In a bottle marked 'white wine vinegar.' It's the stuff the doc prescribed for his anxiety."

"Got it. And I suppose now it's time for you to take me to wardrobe." The sun is creeping up and threatening to start another day of my captivity. I'm unsure how much longer Deputy Candy's natural slumber will last, so I need to get my plan in action *tout de suite*.

Phyllis leads me to the unoccupied bedroom and hovers in front of the closet door.

Turning the handle, I ease open the old door as quietly as possible.

Aaaand my jaw falls open like a cupboard door with one hinge.

If I thought the collection of couture my grandmother amassed for me was shocking, this little closet of horrors is downright chilling. "Holy *Stepford Wives*, Batman!"

The blank look on Phyllis's face makes no connection to my references.

"All right. What would you suggest?"

She puts a dainty hand to her translucent chin and tilts left and right. "Hm, I think with your coloring, that strawberry-cream pink sweater set and the grey skirt will look quite spiffy."

Great, just what I always wanted to be—spiffy.

"I'll take it from here, and you can meet me back downstairs. Let me know if he wakes up." I gesture to the sleeping kidnapper across the hall.

She nods her heart-shaped face and drifts through the wall into the second bedroom.

Putting on the stalker-selected clothing makes my skin crawl. But if I can get out of here—and save Beni—a little discomfort will be worth it. I grab a pair of pink patent-leather kitten heels and carry them as I tiptoe downstairs.

The dull grey dawn is receding as the late-summer sun creeps over the horizon.

Carefully placing a chair in front of the pale-green refrigerator, I step up to retrieve the "white wine vinegar."

Taking a glass from the turquoise cupboard, I pour what I hope is a sufficient dose. I don't want to kill him, but I definitely want to knock him out—for a good, long while.

Adding some water to the bottle, to refill it and hide the evidence of my theft, I replace it in the cabinet with the label turned one-quarter turn to the right, as I found it.

Time to set the table and make some coffee. That smell will probably wake him sooner than later, so I pour a cup, add some sedative, and cover the mug to keep it warm.

Next I scramble some eggs and stir in the last of

the sedative once I take the pan off the heat. Adding a little extra salt and pepper to hide any potential red-flag flavor, I plate up his breakfast and set it on the table as I call loudly upstairs. "Honey, breakfast is on. Hurry up, or your eggs will get cold."

The phrase sickens me, but I have to play my part to the best of my ability. Rustling upstairs gives me a narrow window to scrub out the pan and scramble myself an egg or two—drug-free.

By the time Lane comes downstairs with a shocked expression plastered across his face, I'm sliding my scrambled eggs onto a plate and pouring my coffee.

"Good morning. How did you sleep?"

He's speechless.

Perfect.

"I'm not the best cook, but I'm willing to learn. I hope you like scrambled eggs."

I set his cup of coffee next to his breakfast, and bring my breakfast to the placemat beside his.

"Thanks, Mitzy. The kidnapper must've brought in more supplies while we were asleep. I don't remember seeing eggs in there yesterday. Sure smells good." He takes a bite and nods. "Where did you find those clothes?"

"Oh, you remember, when you told me to search the house. I was just getting so tired of those skinny jeans, I thought a skirt would be nice." At this rate, I'll throw up before I eat my breakfast!

He smiles and leers approvingly. "You look nice."

Ew, and double ew. "Thank you."

Digging into my breakfast with wild abandon, I'm hoping to encourage him to eat fast.

Instead, he savors every bite and drowns me with compliments. "I don't know why you say you're not a good cook. These scrambled eggs are delicious, Mitzy. And the coffee . . . It's out of this world."

Keep talking, psycho. I don't care what you say as long as you drink that coffee in this world!

While he finishes his meal, I clear the table and wash up. "What's on the agenda today? Did you come up with any escape plans? Or were you just teasing, you little scamp?"

He drains the last bit of his coffee, and an evil glee washes over me. "I'll take another look at the items you found and I'm sure I'll come up with something in no time."

"I'm sure you will, my little genius."

A trusting smile reaches from ear to ear across his face, and it almost breaks my heart. However, I immediately remember that he's a creepy stalker kidnapper, and my heart feels absolutely fine. "All right. You work on your project, and I'll be tidying up. How's that sound?"

His smile wavers and his eyes fog. "Sounds good."

That sedative is faster acting than I thought. I pretend not to notice the drowsiness creeping in around the edges, and grab a dishtowel to dry the dishes.

By the time I have the plates and coffee mugs back in the cupboard, Deputy Candy's head drops to the table.

I could move him to a more comfortable location, but I would very much like him to wake up in a puddle of drool and see how he likes it.

In a flash, I race upstairs and slip back into my jeans and T-shirt. If I do manage to escape, I'm not about to be discovered in a sweater set.

Feeling like a superhero back in costume, I grab my trusty oak chair leg—just in case I'm way off and there's an actual kidnapper in the cellar.

When I retrieve my paperclip lock pick and tension wrench from the floorboard right in front of the door, I scoff at Candy's lie. Oh, sure, the kidnapper came in and put eggs in the fridge and then somehow slid my makeshift tools up tight to the door after he left. Blerg! I'm getting pretty sick of him trying to force some kind of Stockholm Syndrome.

The padlock on the basement door is a breeze compared to the contraption installed on the front door.

Racing down the rickety wooden steps, I'm shocked, but not surprised, by what I find. Ben is handcuffed to a post in the middle of the floor, and he looks quite a bit worse for wear. "Beni! Hold on. Let me get you some water."

Back up the stairs, fresh water from the tap, and back down.

He takes a weak sip and chokes.

"Hang in there, buddy. I'm gonna get you out of these handcuffs." Using the paperclip as a distraction, I employ my melting-ice transmutation to open the handcuffs and free him.

He grabs the glass of water with both hands and drains it.

"Have you been down here the whole time? Was he bringing you food? Is there a bathroom?"

A tired smile lifts one corner of Ben's mouth. "Yes, yes, and don't look at that bucket in the corner."

Now that he said it, I can't help but look. "Gross. Let's get you out of here!"

"Did you pick the lock on the front door?"

"Unpickable! Stacked double barrels."

"Wow. That's too much, even for the legendary Mitzy Moon."

"Look, we don't have much time. I have no idea what kind of sedative I'm dealing with, or what is an appropriate dose. Deputy Deranged could wake up any minute."

Picking up my makeshift club from the floor, I push an old wooden crate under one of the narrow basement windows and strike with all my might.

I've never been so happy to hear glass shatter in my entire life. He must have assumed I'd never make it to the basement, so he didn't waste time or money replacing the old panes with Lexan.

"Now what?" Beni gets to his feet and winces.

As I use the sturdy piece of oak to clear out the rest of the glass shards, I bring Ben up to speed on my plan. "Now you get your felonious butt out this window and boost the cop car in the driveway. Take it straight to the main road and radio in. If I know Erick, he already suspects something."

"You want me to steal a cop car?"

"Beni, we've been kidnapped! This is our only chance. Now get over here and shimmy through this window."

He stretches his arms and marches his legs to restore circulation. "What about you?"

"I hate to break it to you, Beni, but there's too much junk in this trunk to fit through that tiny sliver of an opening. You'll have to go for help, and I'll stall him as long as I can."

"How can you stall him? He has a key to the front door."

"Good point. Hold on." Rushing up the open-backed wooden stairs, I shove a paperclip into the door lock and snap it off. He won't be going out through the front door, that's for certain.

Beni is reaching for the small window, but stops. "You sure about this?"

"He won't be able to follow you through that door, and I'll re-secure the padlock once you're out."

"I don't like this plan, Mitzy."

"Too bad. It's the only one we've got. Now go!"

He flicks his black hair to the side, pulls himself up with a surprising burst of strength, and slips through the window with ease. Crouching outside, he calls down to me. "I don't know where we are. How can I call for help if I can't even tell them where we are?"

"I'm sure the squad car has GPS tracking embedded in it somewhere. You just get to the main road and radio for help. Erick will take it from there."

"I'm really starting to regret this scheme, Mitz."

"That makes two of us, Beni."

CHAPTER 12
ERICK

THE FACT THAT I haven't slept a wink since that garage door rolled up and revealed Mitzy's Jeep parked inside isn't the worst news. The worst news is that's the GPS tracker on Deputy Candy's missing patrol car was disabled.

Time that I should've spent sacked out in my rack has instead been wasted, attempting to identify any properties owned by or connected to Deputy Candy or his family. The two places that came up were a vacant lot near Broken Rock, and a small cabin on Fish Lake.

Neither of those places contained a snarky amateur sleuth.

That's an official "no joy."

The door to my office is closed, and I left instructions with dispatch and the deputy at the front desk not to disturb me unless there is an emergency that has to be handled by me personally. No exceptions.

When Deputy Baird bursts through the door, the shock causes me to jump and spill coffee all over my shirt. The upside is that it has been sitting on my desk for so long, it's grown as cold as the rest of my leads. "What the heck, Deputy?"

"You're needed in dispatch! Someone named Benicio Alvarez is calling for you over the radio."

If only I could say how I take a deep breath and calmly walk into dispatch, but I can't. I practically knock Deputy Baird off her feet as I rush past and blast into dispatch like a ton of wayward ordnance. "What've you got?"

She flicks a switch, transferring the transmission from her headset to the speakers, and passes me the mic.

"This is Sheriff Harper. Who's on the line?"

"Hey, it's Ben. You gotta come and get us. That crazy punk deputy kidnapped us!"

My heart is racing. I've trained for scenarios like this my whole life. Not one where a crazy, rogue deputy kidnaps my girlfriend, but high-stress, split-second decisions, every-minute-counts situations. "We can hear you loud and clear, Ben. I need you to stay calm and answer some questions. Are you injured?"

"No. Starving. Got a couple cuts from climbing through the window, but nothing serious."

"10-4. Is Mitzy okay? Is Miss Moon—"

"She's fine. She's working one of her schemes. You know how she gets. She pushed me out that basement window and told me to boost the patrol car. She said you could activate the tracker or something. I don't know where I am."

"10-4. Do you remember how long it took you to get to the location?"

"Bad news there, Harper. He drugged us. But I can tell you about six hours went by—I think—between when we walked out of Final D and when I woke up locked in the basement."

"10-4. That's something. He would've had to make the trip twice, too. He had to come back to Pin Cherry to stash the Jeep back in Mitzy's garage, return to his cruiser at the bar, and drive out to wherever you are."

"He boosted Mitzy's Jeep? She's gonna be salty about that!"

"10-4. Let's get back to figuring out where you are. Any identifying land features? Certain type of tree? Lake? Any road signs?"

"Nothing, man. The trees are nothing special,

but there are a lot of trees. No signs. Um, I drove up a long, dirt road with no houses, then I hit this paved road. Does that help?"

I'd love to tell him it helps about as much as telling me he dropped a needle into a haystack and wants me to recover it, but I need to make sure he stays positive. "Do you think there's any chance you could reconnect the tracker? If you can get that back online, we can ping your location and send help."

"Um, I've only *disconnected* the systems, never turned one back on. But I can give it a try. Where's the transmitter?"

I can't believe I'm about to tell an admitted car thief where the GPS transmitter is on a county law-enforcement vehicle, but I'm running out of options fast.

Turning to the dispatcher, I put my Plan Bravo into action first. "Tell Deputy Paulsen to send four men out to compass points, twenty to thirty minutes outside of town. They'll need to keep an eye to the sky for flares. It's just a backup plan, but they might as well get on the road now."

The dispatcher delivers my orders while I talk Ben through locating the transmitter.

He has his instructions, and if he can locate that tiny plug and reinsert it into the transmitter, we should be able to ping the location and send in the cavalry.

My mind is racing through a series of terrible possibilities as I wait in soul-crushing silence for Ben's report.

"Harper? Sheriff Harper, are you there?"

"Go ahead, Ben."

"I found the transmitter, but someone has ripped the plug and the wires off. If it was a couple loose wires and I had some tools, I might be able to reattach the wires to the box. But the location is real hard to reach and there's no visibility."

"That's okay, Ben. Thanks for trying. Here's the new plan. Pop the trunk, locate the flare gun, and, in about five minutes, shoot off a flare. Continue to fire them straight up into the air at fifteen-minute intervals. I've got deputies moving into position and hopefully one of them will catch sight of your signal. It's not foolproof, but this is all we've got going for us right now. You get set up, and I'll call out the time increments. I'll give you a countdown from three each time, and then you fire. Understood?"

"Yeah, I got it. Let me get set up."

Once again the dead air over the radio is twisting my guts into knots. Somewhere out there the woman I love is a prisoner, and right now there's nothing I can do to save her.

Dispatch reports that the four horsemen are on

the road and will radio in from their lookout points as soon as they're in position.

It's a low-tech solution, a possible waste of manpower, and takes time to put into action. But if I know Mitzy, she can hold her own against Deputy Candy.

"Sheriff?"

"Go ahead, Ben."

"I only have three flares. I hope this works."

"I'm sure it will. Deputy Johnson's out there, and his nickname at the academy was eagle eye. We'll see if he can live up to that today."

"Yeah, if you guys can't find us, I'm gonna take the service revolver and head back to the farmhouse."

Those two pieces of information hit me like a ton of bricks.

Candy doesn't have his gun!

That's a blessing in disguise right there. Somebody up there is definitely looking out for Mitzy today. Plus, Ben described the property as a farmhouse. I've been looking for hunting cabins and old homestead shacks. "That's good news about the gun, Ben. But I don't want you to do anything stupid. There's no guarantee that Candy doesn't have a backup piece at the property. Did you say it was a farmhouse?"

"Yeah, I only saw the basement from the inside,

but from the outside, it's a two-story farmhouse. Looks pretty small, and it's in the middle of a lot of acreage. No neighbors in any direction. Oh, and there were a ton of old rusty tools in the basement. And some horseshoes."

"That's great. That's really great information. I'm gonna turn over the countdowns to dispatch and go back through the property records. You gave me some good intel, Ben. Sit tight. We'll find you."

Dispatch takes over, counting down to the flare discharges, and I head back toward my office.

Farmhouse. Possibly owned by a black-smith/farmer. Single dwelling on a large piece of property. I might be able to work with this.

The new set of clues has reinvigorated me, and I'm allowing myself a flicker of hope. When I round the corner into my office, the sight of Silas Willoughby stops me short.

"Good morning, Sheriff Harper. It is my belief that Miss Moon is not on a road trip. May I be of assistance?"

A weary smile eases the tension in my jaw. Between you and me, I've always known this man was far more than he seems. The way he took Mitzy under his wing when she got to town only confirms my belief in those possibilities. "Tell you what, Silas, your timing couldn't be better. I just got off the horn with that Benicio Alvarez character and he describes a remote farm property on a large plot, possibly owned by a blacksmith. I have some plat maps. Maybe you could assist me in going through them to locate a property or two that matches that description?"

The elderly man respectfully rises and nods his head. He smooths his glorious grey mustache and reaches into the pocket of his singular tweed coat. "I can do you one better, Sheriff. Are you familiar with pendulums?"

Suspicion confirmed. "Mitzy introduced me to them. What do you need from me?"

"I believe a county map would suffice."

Reaching into a file drawer in the handy metal cabinet behind my desk, I hastily grab a map and spread it across a flat surface.

"What is it that you wish to ascertain, Sheriff?"

"I want to find Mitzy."

"Indeed. We should like to know the precise location of Mizithra Achelois Moon, right now." Mr. Willoughby extends his gnarled hands over the map, drops the pendulum, and allows it to still. Then he repeats the question aloud a second time, and the conical stone at the end of the antique bronze chain quivers.

It swings in wide arcs from left to right, circles three times, and then the spirals tighten toward the western edge of Birch County.

Suddenly the point of the inverted cone lunges toward a spot on the map and sticks as if it were pulled by a magnet. I don't know what powers are at work, but if they help me find Mitzy, I don't much care.

"It has selected Maple Grove as the answer to our question." Mr. Willoughby carefully replaces the pendulum into a hidden pocket.

Depressing the button on my mic, I call into dispatch. "Deputy Paulsen, who's holding the west?"

"That'd be Johnson, Sheriff Harper. You want me to bring him in?"

"Negative. Send him toward Maple Grove and tell him to keep the windows down."

"10-4."

A call to dispatch confirms that two flares have been fired, and the next will go in fourteen minutes.

If this pendulum thingy is right, then Deputy Johnson may not have seen the last flare, but he'll hopefully be within sight of the next one.

The last one.

"Is there any additional area in which I may assist, Sheriff?"

"Not at this time, Silas. I have a deputy en route to this location. If she's there—" My traitorous voice cracks and the old man places a comforting hand on my shoulder.

"Don't lose faith, Sheriff. The Mitzy Moon that

you and I know would never let a *noob* like Deputy Candy get the best of her."

His use of the pop culture term, which he surely learned from Miss Moon, brings some much-needed laughter to the room.

He's right. Mitzy is so much more than meets the eye.

"I shall endeavor to meet you and Miss Moon for breakfast at the diner tomorrow morning. I feel there will be much to discuss." Mr. Willoughby smooths his mustache and exits without waiting for my reply.

If only I had that kind of faith. At times like this, it's hard to keep the ugly memories of war—

"Sheriff! Deputy Johnson saw the last flare. He's headed to the location now, and Paulsen directed the other deputies to join him. It's someplace called 'Anderson's Farrier.' Been abandoned for decades, according to our records."

The relief is instantly swallowed by a mammoth surge of adrenaline. "10-4, Baird. I'm en route."

I've never driven the cruiser this fast, but every second counts. I can feel it in my bones. "This is Sheriff Harper. All units approach Code 2 and take up standard 'barricaded with a hostage' positions. Hold for my arrival. Do not make contact or reveal your positions. I repeat: do not make contact."

A series of 10-4s cascade over the radio and I

push the gas pedal to the floor. Having them approach without the lights or sirens may buy us a few precious minutes. Once Candy realizes he's been discovered—

Hang on, Mitzy. Just hang on a little while longer . . .

CHAPTER 13

ANY PASSING FANCY I had about being an actress is absolutely cured. The work is too hard and the wardrobe is suffocating. I'm back in my sweater set, skirt, and kitten heels, pretending to be in a drugged stupor in bedroom number two.

The sedative I gave Candy finally wears off, and I track his movements with my standard issue ears and an extra scoop of psychic perceptions.

When he first awakes, his heart is racing. He stumbles downstairs and checks the front door and the basement door. Satisfied that they are still secure, he comes upstairs and takes a leisurely shower.

What a jerk! If I knew where the water heater was, I'd go and turn it off.

Next, he returns to the kitchen and makes himself some drug-free food. However, when he attempts to use his key to exit the front door, good little "Candy, Lane" emits a stream of expletives.

This pleases me greatly. I may not be able to get out of this place, but now, neither can he!

He must be looking out the window, because the psychic jolt of pure terror that shoots up the stairs nearly knocks me off the bed.

Once he makes the missing-car discovery, he tries the padlock and finds it jammed as well.

Seems like the perfect time for me to make my Donna Reed entrance.

"Good morning, Lane. How did you sleep?"

He's immediately suspicious, but my messy hair and crumpled skirt seem to temporarily confuse him. "It was fine. I slept fine."

"Can I make you a sandwich?"

"No." He rubs his hands over his face and softens his tone. "No, thank you. I'm not hungry."

"Oh dear, it sounds like someone ate a bowl of cold gorilla biscuits. What can we do to turn that frown upside down?" This version of playacting is lifting my spirits a fraction of an inch.

"It's nothing. I just thought maybe, you know, whoever kidnapped us would've brought us more supplies. But I didn't see anything, so maybe we should—"

"Start rationing?" I let my eyes widen in mock terror.

"What? Rationing? No, I was going to say figure out an escape plan."

I clap my hands together like a *Toddlers & Tiaras* mom. "Oh, goody. I love plans."

He narrows his gaze and eyes me suspiciously. "How long was I out?"

As I mentioned, my acting is barely passable. I'm clearly playing this character a little too perky. "Oh, I have no idea. I was asleep myself."

"Then who jammed the lock on the front door?"

Oops. Plot hole. What now?

"Oh, that was totally me. I just wanted to give the lock one more try. But I started getting so sleepy, I probably turned the pick too hard. Sorry about that. But the good news is, now the kidnapper can't get back in, right?" I bat my eyelashes in a way that nauseates me, and hug my hands to my chest hopefully.

My clairsentience picks up on Candy's inner turmoil. He's struggling with the idea of maintaining his co-captive status or revealing his true intentions. The longer I can keep him convinced that we're in this thing together, the better off I'll be. "Do you think maybe they paid the ransom, and

Ben decided not to come back? What if he's going to leave us here to starve?"

Relief melts across Lane's face, and he nods as he speaks. "That makes sense. My cruiser's missing from the driveway. Maybe he did decide to take the money and run. It would be better for him to get out of town, before he revealed our location."

And just like that, I've got my captor eating out of my hand. "That's sort of good news. But now we really need to find a way out." I click across the speckled linoleum in my kitten heels and lean over the scant row of items on the table.

Lane approaches from my left and stands uncomfortably close. "There's just not much to work with, Mitzy. You tried breaking the windows, and all you got for your trouble was a bump on the head."

"I've got an idea! I don't know why I didn't think of this before." Grabbing the ball of twine and the matches, I hurry toward the fireplace.

My increasingly concerned captor follows close behind. "What are you gonna do?"

"I'm going to put this shattered chair into the fireplace, wrap some twine around a couple of these legs, and light it on fire! Somebody has to be out looking for us by now. They'll see the smoke from the chimney, and maybe come to check it out."

He grips my wrist and shakes his head. "We

don't know anything about this old place. The chimney could be backed up and you'll fill the whole house with smoke. We could die of smoke inhalation."

I don't care for the way he's squeezing my wrist. "Lane, you're hurting me."

Where I expected regret, a strange satisfaction clouds his features. There is darkness beneath his boyish exterior, and I don't want it to come out to play.

Before I can wrench my wrist free from his tightening grip, Phyllis appears behind him with her ethereal vacuum in tow.

The words are out of my mouth before my brain engages. "Were you buried with your vacuum?"

Phyllis continues to move the flickering appliance methodically across the carpet as she repeats her mantra. "A woman's work is never done. A woman's work is never done. A woman's work is never done."

Lane drops my wrist and steps away. "What did you say?"

Think. Think. Think. "I think it's a line from a movie. It's really not that funny if you haven't seen it. Never mind."

He backs up two more paces and passes through the apparition of Phyllis. I recognize the ghost-chill bumps on his arms. Lane stops moving and his eyes go wild. "Is it cold in here? Did you feel it get really cold?"

Fortunately, my arms are covered in pale-pink angora so he can't see my ghost-immune skin. But I fake shiver and rub them firmly all the same. "Yeah. It's freezing. I really think we should start a fire."

He steps farther away, but he's still completely freaked.

Eager to take advantage of his distraction, I wrap two chair legs with twine, pile the broken chair in the fireplace, and reach up to open the flue.

Yes, I know all about flues. I worked at a ski re-sort in Flagstaff one winter as a runner for the on-site restaurant, and, even though I was only sup-posed to deliver food, guests always had plenty of other chores for me to do once I entered the room.

The first match fizzles out before I can get it to the twine. I move the matchbox closer and hold the twine right beside the striking surface. Match number two burns a second longer, blackens the twine, but fails to ignite. Match number three—suc-cess! The twine is burning on one leg, but as I move to repeat the process on the other chair leg, Candy snaps out of his trance.

Lane lunges forward and knocks the matchbook from my hand. He grips my shoulders tightly and pushes me toward the sofa.

I put my hands up and shout, "Take it easy."

He races to the kitchen and returns with a glass of water, dousing the meager flames flickering around the first chair leg and sending a weak puff of white smoke up the chimney. Certainly nothing that would draw anyone's attention.

"Lane! Why did you do that? The smoke could've helped someone find us."

His demeanor changes in the blink of an eye. Gone is the accommodating co-captive. Now the brilliant but demented kidnapper emerges. "I know what you're doing, Mitzy, and it won't work. How long have you known the truth?"

I slip off the kitten heels and throw them across the room at the vacuuming ghost. "*Know?* Not until you tried to convince me that the kidnapper had visited us, when my makeshift lock pick set was still pressed up against the bottom of the front door. But I suspected from the very beginning. You made a pretty good argument for Beni needing money, but he's just not that kind of guy. He doesn't have a hidden dark side—like some people."

"You brought this on yourself, Mitzy. I planned the perfect home for us. But I was willing to wait. I even started to talk myself out of loving you when I saw how much you cared about Sheriff Harper. But when you went gallivanting around town on a drunken bender with some loser from out of state, I knew you didn't feel the same way about the sheriff as he did about you."

My breath is coming in shallow shudders. If memory serves, this is the part of the movie when it's in the victim's best interest to keep the crazy guy talking for as long as possible. "You don't know how I feel about Erick. Beni's just a friend. I wasn't cheating on Erick."

"No more excuses, Mitzy. We're going to make this work. I just need you to take a little nap while I call a locksmith to come out here and change the lock on the front door. Then things will return to normal. You can cook for me, keep the house neat and tidy, and I'll bring you anything you need."

It's do or die time, and I'm gonna *do*! "Is that what your great-grandfather told Phyllis?"

The color slowly drains from his face, until his complexion nearly matches that of the manic housekeeping ghost. "What are you talking about? No one knows about Phyllis."

"Well, you seem to know about her, and I know about her. So, at least two people know about Phyllis."

"My grandfather tried to take care of her. She wasn't— She suffered from mental illness."

Phyllis switches off the vacuum, meticulously winds up the cord, and screams to the heavens.

"I don't think Phyllis suffered from mental illness. I think your great-grandfather drove her crazy. That's what being locked up in a house, and not being able to visit your family, or play bridge with your friends, or get your own groceries will do to a woman."

Phyllis floats toward me and sends another wave of ghost chills through Lane. "And he took my son. You tell him that! He took my son."

"I suppose when your great-grandfather took her only child away, that was the final nail in the coffin."

Lane's eyes are a dangerous mix of fear and anger. "Where are you getting this information? My grandfather changed his name. He changed his son's name. There's no connection between the present day Candys and this house—or Phyllis."

"Oh, Phyllis told me herself."

He takes a giant step backward and crashes into the wall. "Impossible! Phyllis disappeared. No one ever found her. By now she's dead. Long dead. You're making all this up."

I'd love to go upstairs and get back into my skinny jeans and a T-shirt for this dénouement, but it looks like I'm going to have to play "tough girl" in a sweater set. "If she's long dead, and she just disappeared, why are you getting so agitated? It seems like what I'm saying might be closer to the truth than you'd like to admit. Maybe the *crazy* skipped a generation or two and you've got the same disorder as your great-grandfather. The difference is, Lane, I'm not going to be your Phyllis."

The ghost swirls back and forth in front of me in a panic. "Don't say that, dear. Don't agitate him."

"Is that what went wrong with Phyllis? Did she try to stand up for herself? That Easter Sunday back in 1959 when she put on her best dress and her prettiest hat—"

"Stop saying these things! You don't know what you're talking about. Phyllis disappeared."

"What if she didn't disappear, Lane? What if your great-grandfather strangled her in this house and then buried her in the basement to hide the evidence?"

Lane is definitely coming unhinged. I don't know how this disaster is going to end, but I'm afraid— Hold the phone! Did he say he wanted me to take a nap so he could *call* a locksmith? If he's going to call someone, that means there's a phone in this house. I might not be able to outrun him, but I hope I can outsmart him! "I'm sorry if I upset you. Sometimes I hear voices, all right? I need to use the restroom."

He moves to block the door, but I lower my shoulder and ram through. Running up the stairs, I dart sharply into the bedroom he's been using, slam the door and wedge a rickety chair under the handle. The phone has to be in this room somewhere.

Loud banging at the door is a bad sign. "Mitzy! What are you doing?"

As I rip the sheets off the bed and pillowcases off the pillows, I attempt to sound ill. "I don't feel well. I need to lie down." Cough. Cough. Groan.

Nothing. No phone.

I need to calm down and focus. I'll never be able to find that phone if I can't tap into my extra senses.

The handle jiggles sharply and the strikes against the door become more forceful.

Closing my eyes, I place both hands on my abdomen and slow my breathing. Where is the phone? It's not under the mattress.

The chair is squeaking, and it's likely going to give way.

My clairaudience picks the word *Bible* out of the air, and I race to the nightstand. The drawer is empty!

The chair against the door is not long for this world.

My eyes search the surfaces and stop on a hand-carved cradle under the window.

I rip the tiny quilt back and see an old family Bible. Yanking it upward it falls open, and my phone slides to the floor.

I lunge toward the prize as the chair splinters.

The phone is in my hand when Lane wrenches the door open.

At the very moment I fear my life will flash before my eyes, the sweetest sound in all the world blares through the Lexan windows.

CHAPTER 14
ERICK

"DEPUTY CANDY, this is Sheriff Harper. We have the place surrounded. You know this drill better than most. I'd like you to come out and peaceably surrender. Let's talk about this. Man to man."

A hostage situation is a lawman's worst nightmare. We have a thirty-four percent chance of successful rescue. And that's if no one starts shooting.

I'm hoping to see Mitzy appear in one of the windows, but there's no immediate response. Then a loud crash from the second floor concerns me.

Motioning for the deputies to fan out, I depress the button on the megaphone. "Deputy Candy, let's keep this professional. So far there has been no loss of life and no charges brought. Maybe we have ourselves a misunderstanding. The sooner you come out and clear things up the better it will be for you."

My cell phone rings, and I set the bullhorn down with irritation. When I see the name pop up on Caller ID, my heart constricts. I hit the speaker icon and cross my fingers. "Mitzy, is it really you?"

"Hey, Erick, is that a new bullhorn I hear?"

It would be highly unprofessional for me to cry in front of my deputies, so I take the huge ball of emotion wedged in my throat and stuff it down as hard as I can. "So that crash I heard, that was Candy?"

"10-4. 'Candy, Lane' took a nasty spill down the stairs when he tried to repossess my phone. I'm currently locked in the one and only bathroom, and thought you might like an update."

"Are you okay?" My voice catches.

"I'll let you decide for yourself when you see what I am wearing, Sheriff."

Despite the churning in my gut, this woman always finds a way to make me laugh. "I can't wait. Are you able to open the front door?"

"That's a negatory, good buddy. My brilliant captor locked us inside, and I'm not about to go digging for the key. Plus, I broke off a paperclip in the lock so Lane couldn't go after Beni when I shoved him out the basement window. Beni's all right, isn't he?"

"He's great. He led us right to you." Boy, these

waterworks are really itching to spill. "Are you sure Candy is unarmed?"

Her satisfied scoff warms my heart. "Not only is he unarmed, Sheriff, but he's currently unconscious. Who knows for how long? Seems like psychos have a knack for reanimating faster than expected. And FYI, the windows are all bulletproof, and, if you were wondering, I'm not able to fit out of the basement window."

"No problem. Standby. I'll send the deputies in with the battering ram. Keep safe in that bathroom until I give you the all clear. Copy?"

"Copy that, Sheriff Harper."

My deputies have already suited up in Kevlar and helmets. They pull out the battering ram and approach the door in formation. I take a position to the side, draw my weapon and hope I don't have to shoot a sadly misguided young man.

The battering ram meets serious resistance in the recently upgraded front door, but the much older wood of the doorjamb finally gives way, and within minutes the deputies have breached the farmhouse.

Paulsen is the first to enter.

She calls over the radio, "Kitchen, clear."

The remaining officers enter.

Paulsen on the mic. "There's a body at the base of the staircase. Cover me, Johnson."

Any additional communication is conducted deputy to deputy inside the dwelling.

Paulsen steps onto the front porch and waves the paramedics in. "We've got him in cuffs, Sheriff. He's alive, a little woozy, but coming around. We'll let the paramedics get him on a board, and Gilbert can ride along to the hospital."

I rise with a sigh of relief, and holster my weapon. "10-4. Good job in there."

Returning to my cruiser, I grab the bullhorn off the hood and make an announcement. "Mitzy Moon, all clear. Please exit the dwelling."

A slightly dazed woman in a pink sweater and grey skirt stumbles through the remains of the front entrance. If it wasn't for that snow-white hair and unmistakable grin, I would've had no idea what I was looking at. "Mitzy!" I close the distance between us as quickly as possible and, when I pull her into my arms, she fires off one of her classic lines.

"So what do you think of 'Candy, Lane's' fashion sense?" She gestures to her costume.

My arms wrap around her, and I can't hold her tight enough. All thought of my sheriff's duties vanish as I inhale her rich eucalyptus scent and struggle to swallow. I'll be honest, a couple of tears leak onto her stupid fuzzy sweater.

Ben stops in his tracks, smiles at me, and nods. He walks quietly back to the car.

I've been the third wheel a few times myself, and I admire a guy who knows when he's been beat and takes it in stride. Maybe I rushed to judgment where Alvarez is concerned. That's a problem for another time. Right now, I can't get enough of my firecracker of a girlfriend. "So glad you're okay. For a minute, I really did think you went on a road trip."

She pulls away and her intelligent grey eyes gaze up at me as her soft thumb wipes a tear from my jaw. "Road trip? When did I go on a road trip?"

"I'm sure if you check your text history, you'll see that Lane was feeding me a bunch of crap to keep me from looking for you."

She shakes her head and shivers uncontrollably. "He's been planning this for a long time, Erick. The way he outfitted this house, how he changed up his plan, and the supply of sedatives—"

I have to kiss her full lips and stop the flow of information. Later, when we're alone, I'll let her tell the entire story. Right now I can't bear to hear how close I came to losing her. "Glad you're safe. I'm sure your grandmother is worried sick. We better get you back to the bookshop. And we have a breakfast date with Silas."

"Silas? Does he know I'm missing?"

Savoring my brief moment of being a quarter of a step ahead of her, I tilt my head and stroke a thumb along my jaw, just to make her wait a beat.

"You know Silas; he's more than meets the eye. Between the piece of fabric Pyewacket ripped off the deputy's uniform pants, and Silas and his magic pendulum, we got to you just in time."

She smiles and sighs. "That fiendish feline! He'll never let me hear the end of it."

"And let's not shortchange Silas. Maybe someday you'll tell me more about that man's true profession. I've never met a lawyer with such a gift for unraveling the paranormal."

Mitzy drags her fingers across her lips and twists them in front with an invisible key. Of course, a second later her mouth is right back at work. "I'm going to run upstairs and get my actual clothes, but I'll leave this get up on until I get back to the library. Grams will think it's a real hoot."

She turns toward the house and my eyes drink in her every curve.

When she looks back over her shoulder, there's a palpable hint of fear in her eyes.

"Erick, will you come with me? I don't think I can go back in by myself. You know?"

I'm at her side in a flash, and we retrieve her clothes. She even lets one of the deputies know where to collect the remaining liquid sedative for evidence.

Back outside, I head toward my car and wave her along. "Come on, let's get out of here."

"Honestly, I'd love to make a run for it, but I have some—" she leans in close and whispers "—ghost business to attend to."

I tilt my head and lift one eyebrow. "With your grandmother?"

Mitzy chews the inside of her cheek for a second. "Um, no. According to Phyllis Anderson, Lane's great-grandmother, she was murdered. Her ghost is gonna be trapped here until the truth comes out about what her husband did."

There's so much of this ghost stuff that I don't understand—can't understand. She must read the doubt on my face.

"Hey, I owe her, Erick. If she hadn't told me about what happened in the past, I never would've gotten the upper hand with Lane. I promised her I'd make sure the right people heard her story. Is there some way you can clear the deputies out of the house for a few minutes and let me do my paranormal interpreter thing?"

This is a big ask. Maybe if I get some circulation to my brain, it will clear away these shadows. I turn and pace in the dirt driveway for a couple of minutes before offering her a hopeful smile. "I think I've got an angle. Sit tight."

She tugs at the edges of her skirt and offers me a curtsy.

"Paulsen, can you clear everyone out of the

house? I need to have Miss Moon walk me through the events while they're still fresh in her mind. I think it will be easier for her if there are no distractions."

Paulsen adjusts her duty belt and sucks air sharply through her teeth. "10-4, Sheriff."

A moment later she's executed the orders, and re-assigned the remaining deputies on site.

Mitzy and I re-enter the dwelling, and her little pink shoes tap across the kitchen into the living room.

Having no idea what we're looking for, I blindly tag along. "Is she here? This ghost of Phyllis Anderson?"

"Don't take that tone with me, Erick. I'm no spirit expert. Maybe it's a *Beetlejuice* thing." Mitzy takes a deep breath and intones, "Phyllis Anderson. Phyllis Anderson. Phyllis Anderson."

I cross my arms and wait, like a high schooler playing "Bloody Mary" at a sleepover. Of course, I'm assuming again. Guys don't really do the "sleepover" thing.

Mitzy's eyes widen next to me, and she steps back. "Phyllis, this is Sheriff Harper. I told him your story, but we need some kind of evidence—" A hand covers her mouth and she shakes her head in horror.

The look concerns me, and I lean toward her.

"What is it? What did the ghost tell you?" It's awful hard for me to believe in any of this, but all I really have to do is believe in Mitzy, and that's not too tough.

She places a shaky hand on her stomach. "Phyllis said she's buried in the basement."

I rake my fingers through my hair and struggle to get the loose hairs out of my eyes. "What? I can't ask people to dig up the basement floor for no reason. Can she show you where?"

Mitzy gazes off at an empty space several feet in front of her and asks, "Can you, Phyllis? It would be a huge help." There's a brief pause, and she continues, "Follow me, Erick. She's going to take us to the gravesite."

After retrieving a crowbar from the trunk of my cruiser, and snapping the jammed padlock off the basement door, I let Mitzy lead the way.

The cement of the old basement floor is rough and unprofessionally done. The curious thing is that when Mitzy points out the spot where the ghost claims her body is buried, there's a visible demarcation between the older concrete and the new pour, which allegedly covers Phyllis's grave. It gives me something to work with. "Okay. I'll cook up some story—"

Mitzy lunges forward and grips my arm. "I know! You can say that Ben told you. That Deputy

Candy was sharing some of his family history to scare Ben into cooperating and mentioned the buried grandmother. No one can check. Right?"

Not for the first time, I'm relieved this beautiful genius of a woman is on my team. "That actually might work."

Her smile melts my heart. "Thanks for that, Sheriff."

"Now it's time to get you out of here. Should I drive you straight to Myrtle's Diner?"

Mitzy swallows hard and shakes her head. "I need to see Grams first."

I slide my arm around her shoulders and squeeze. "Mitzy Moon is saying no to fries. You're more traumatized than I thought."

She snuggles close and draws a shaky breath. "Maybe I am, but I feel better now that you're here."

Leaving Deputy Paulsen in charge of the crime scene, I help Mitzy into the passenger seat of my vehicle, and drive back toward Pin Cherry as though I have all the time in the world.

Someday, I'm going to figure out how to make sure this amazing woman spends all her spare time with me, but today I'll simply revel in our victory, and hold her sweet hand.

CHAPTER 15

No sooner do I open the side door than Grams blasts into and through me. "Mitzy! I was worried sick! What happened?"

I wrap my arms clumsily around her ethereal form, and the last of my escape-plan adrenaline boost drains away as though someone pulled the stopper from a tub.

Turning to my rescuer with an embarrassed grin, I let my arms fall to my sides. "Can you give me a little time to freshen up and fill in Grams?"

Erick's broad shoulders shrug, and he offers me half a grin. "I'm not crazy about leaving you alone after that place I just pulled you out of, but I'm pretty sure you're safe now. Can I bring you some lasagna and breadsticks from Angelo and Vinci's for dinner? There's going to be a heckuva lot of paperwork, so it'll likely be on the late side, but I'd like to —you know—hang out with you tonight." The flush on his cheeks is everything.

Placing a hand on my hip, I grin mischievously. "On one condition."

He shakes his head and playfully puts a hand over his eyes. "You don't skip a beat, do you?"

"I do not. I will allow dinner to be delivered by Sheriff Too-Hot-To-Handle, if I'm allowed to observe the interrogation with Lane Candy tomorrow."

Erick crosses his arms in that yummy way that makes his biceps bulge and nods. "Deal. You want to be in the room?"

My skin crawls underneath the itchy angora. "Ew. No thanks. I'd prefer to hang out in the observation room, but I'll knock on the window if I think you miss any of the important facts."

He laughs. "I have no doubt. By the way, Deputy Gilbert took Alvarez to the hospital. You might want to pay Ben a visit after you're finished here."

"Thanks. And thanks for trusting me. I hope you get that Beni is just an old friend—nothing more. I don't give my heart away in pieces, Sheriff. I'm an all-or-nothing girl."

The emotion that he's been holding back threatens to burst forth. He leans forward, gives me a quick peck on the cheek, and practically sprints back to his squad car.

His citrus-woodsy scent lingers in the air and my heart flutters when I think about "hanging out" with him tonight.

Upstairs in my swanky apartment, I collapse onto the four-poster bed and snuggle around an uncooperative Pyewacket. While Grams is critiquing my stalker's fashion choices, I whisper my gratitude in a black-tufted ear. "And once again, you are the smartest, most resourceful, most beautiful kitten in all the world."

"Reow." Can confirm.

He pretends to be mad, but as I scratch his head and rake my fingers through his fur, he's powerless to resist. A low purr shakes the bed.

"All right. I'm going to take an embarrassingly long, ridiculously hot shower and then we can discuss your murder wall, Isadora."

Grams smirks and glides a finger along one of her perfectly drawn brows. "I learned from the best. I tell you what, sweetie: if Sheriff Harper had come to me sooner, we'd have had you home hours earlier."

"Oh, and you're humble too."

She laughs so hard she snorts, and I disappear into the bathroom to peel off my sweater set, skirt, and kitten heels. I deposit them directly into the trashcan. Sure, I could've donated them, but I don't think they deserve a second life.

The glorious, steamy shower and the revitalizing eucalyptus bath products breathe new life into my weary body and soul.

When I emerge with one towel wrapped around my head and another around my aching body, Ghost-ma is swirling in front of her 3 x 5 cards.

"Finally! I thought I'd cross over before you came out of that shower."

Collapsing on the bed, next to my four-legged hero, I spill out the tale of my kidnapping, ghost whispering, and rescue.

Yes, there are multiple interruptions. No, they're not all from Grams. Pye insisted on hearing the bit about how he helped Erick at least twice.

Grams floats distractedly near the 6 x 6 windows and she's sniffling.

"What's wrong? I made it back safe."

"I know, dear. What if you hadn't? You're all I've got. I'm sure Twiggy would carry on running the bookshop, but that's no real legacy. You know what I mean."

I'm suddenly afraid I know exactly what she means. "Are you insinuating something about great grandchildren?"

Her shimmering eyes widen in mock inno-
cence. "What?"

"Wow! You're gonna need to simmer down.
Erick and I are in an absolutely wonderful place in
our relationship. Things are moving at the exact
right speed, and your unnecessary shovings will not
push this great thing I have off the rails."

"I wasn't pushing—"

"Oh, puh-leeeeeze. I feel like you've probably
been pushing since the day you were born. That's
likely where I get it from, but it doesn't make it
right. Now, I'm going to march myself down to
Myrtle's Diner and gorge on whatever that wonderful man puts in front of me. I'll be back before
you know it. Single, unmarried, and UN-knocked-
up. Understood?"

She pops one of her sarcastic salutes, and I roll
my eyes as I stride across the Rare Books Loft, in-
haling the comforting scent of endless possibilities.

Back in my regulation skinny jeans and high
tops, I slide my precious one-of-a-kind triangular
brass key underneath my T-shirt as I exit the bookstore. Today's T-shirt selection pictures a roaring
bear with a sign: "Approach at Your Own Risk."

Outside the intricately carved wooden door that
serves as the front entrance to my bookshop, I pause
and run my fingers over the detailed vignettes: a
centaur chasing a maiden through delicate wood-

land; a faun playing a flute for a family of rabbits dancing around his cloven feet; the shadow of a winged horse passing in front of the moon; a wildcat stalking a small boy—a cat who bears a striking resemblance to Pyewacket.

Silas was pretty cagey when I asked him about that cat. Maybe one day I'll manage to get enough brandy down that man's gullet to loosen his wizened tongue.

The sun feels warmer, clouds float like pure white puffs of cotton candy, and the gulls swooping over the glistening lake seem to call out my name. I made the right choice to stay in Pin Cherry Harbor.

The life I had in Arizona was a scrabbling act of survival. This place pulled out the best in me and uncovered hidden talents that I may never have found if I'd remained in the Southwest. I'll always have fond memories of the wonderful life my mother provided for me, until fate stole her away, but I'm so much happier making all these fresh memories right here.

The door of the diner gives way under my hand, but the tableau that greets me couldn't have been predicted by the best of psychics.

No joke.

The quaint diner is jam-packed with patrons.

Must be up for the baking competition. See, I've learned a few things since I landed in town.

Tatum is hustling from table to table with a pitcher of water in her right hand and a pitcher of iced tea in her left. Her mother Tally is behind the grill and smiles warmly at me through the orders-up window.

Her sister Tilly is away from the bank and out of her functional heels for the first time in recent memory. She's wearing an apron and apparently waiting tables.

Nowhere in this entire scene do I see the familiar grey buzz cut of Odell Johnson.

Grabbing the last stool at the counter, I slide in and offer a confused wave to the substitute cook.

Tilly scampers over with her poof of grey-blonde hair backcombed to perfection. She pulls the pencil from behind her ear. "What can I getcha, hon?"

"Hi Tilly. Where's Odell?"

She leans back and squints. A huge smile lifts her doughy round cheeks as recognition seeps in. "Mitzy! So sorry, dear. I'm running around like a chicken with my head cut off here and I barely looked at your face. Odell's taking his usual two days off for the competition. Since the bank is closed on weekends, I've always helped out, and Tally is a pro at the grill."

"Oh. I'll have a burger and fries. And soda, I mean, pop."

She scribbles on her pad and lays the ticket on the little shelf spanning the bottom of the window into the kitchen.

His usual two days off? I have no recollection of Odell ever taking five minutes off. Although, to be fair, I was a little wrapped up in my own nonsense when I first got to town, so it stands to reason that I may have missed a detail here or there. Now that I think about it, I do remember him saying something about winning the Pin Cherry pie contest every year except 1984. Is that right?

Tatum slides a soda in front of me and leans down to whisper conspiratorially. "I hear you got another one."

"What?"

"You know. Cracked another case and the sheriff arrested another bad guy. It's all anyone's talking about." A strand of her curly red hair has wiggled loose from her high pony, and she tucks it behind her ear.

Since I'm barely three hours safe, the speed of the Pin Cherry gossip *wireless* surprises even me. Taking a page from my mother's book, I nod and smile.

Tatum winks and hurries off to attend to other customers.

I really wish Odell was here. I was eager to see what he thought the perfect post-kidnapping meal would be, but I also know I can't go wrong with a juicy burger and delicious golden fries.

Despite the chaos in the diner, Tally personally delivers my plate. "Here you go, sweetie. I know Odell would've wanted you to have a milkshake. Is chocolate all right?"

I gaze at the glorious frosty fountain glass and grin as wide as the Grand Canyon. "You're an angel! That's exactly what I needed!"

She leans down and scrunches up her nose as she smiles. "I gave you extra whip, and two cherries."

"Whatever he's paying you, it's not enough, Tally."

She shrugs her shoulders, adjusts the pencil stabbed into her tightly wound flame-red topknot, and hustles back to the grill.

The addition of the chocolate milkshake adds almost two full minutes to my normal four-minute eating time, but it's worth every slurp.

I grab my dishes and drop them into the bus bin behind the counter. Waving to the three Sikanen gals as I leave, I realize I have to break my promise to Grams. Even though I told her I'd be back in a flash, I definitely have to go to the hospital before I get pulled into any more of her surreptitious relationship plans.

Shoot! I left my keys with Lars. And if Erick found the Jeep tucked back in my garage, "Candy, Lane" must've hotwired my precious baby! Throwing my hands up in the air, I stop in the middle of the alley as frustration washes over me.

But suddenly a lightbulb pings to life above my head. "The Mercedes!"

Punching in the code, I hear the song from *Ferris Bueller's Day Off* as the garage rolls up to reveal my silver beauty. "Oh, yeah!"

I wish the drive to the hospital was longer. I forgot how flipping awesome it is to drive this fabulous set of wheels.

Reluctantly pulling into a visitor spot, I let the gullwing door float up, and I lovingly pat the steering wheel as I slide out.

Deputy Gilbert walks across the parking lot toward his cruiser as I approach the Birch County Regional Medical Facility.

"Hey, Deputy Gilbert. Is Mr. Alvarez all right?"

He glances in my direction, bites his bottom lip for a second, and smiles. "Yeah. Yeah, I think so. They ran a lot of tests, and I had to hang out to get his statement. He's in room 214. I left your name with the nurse's station, per Sheriff

Harper's orders. You should be able to head right in."

"Thanks." I wave as he pulls away from the hospital. He seems a little off somehow, but it must've hit all the deputies pretty hard that one of their own turned. I wish I could give him some perfect explanation as to how Candy slipped through the cracks and ended up with a badge. Sadly, the truth is that systems are only as good as the people who run them. After all, Candy is a verified genius.

My innate distrust of hospitals has softened since my time in almost-Canada. Turns out that there are a lot of good-hearted people working hard to save lives in these places. The anxiety and fear that built up during my youth seems to have much more to do with a general lack of finances and information than any legitimate medical shortcomings.

Beni's room isn't hard to find, and once I give my name to the nurse that stops me in the corridor, I'm given free rein.

"Hey, Beni, how you doing?"

He turns his head on the stark white pillow and reaches for the hospital bed remote. Once he adjusts himself to a more comfortable sitting position, he smiles and shakes his head. "You and that sheriff are pretty deep in it, aren't you?"

The question brings a flood of self-conscious heat to my cheeks. "I guess. I don't know."

"Mitz, it's me you're talking to. We saw each other through some dark days, you know. I remember that desperate, terrified look that used to lurk in your eyes. It's gone. When I saw you two— after the thing at the farmhouse . . ."

"Beni, why are you doing this to me?"

"No, no. I don't mean anything. I'm happy for you, Mitz. I swear. You deserve the absolute best life you can possibly get your hands on. After all your childhood stuff, you know."

I reach out and place my hand on his arm, just above the IV needle secured with tape to the back of his hand. "Thanks, Beni. I didn't say it before, but back in the bad old days . . . Thanks for always being there for me. I think you're the only real friend I ever had."

His eyes shine and a smile tugs up one side of his mustache. "Yeah, we were always better friends than lovers."

A calm silence hangs between us, and I can sense the memories bouncing around in both of our heads. When I left Arizona behind me, it was easy to vilify all of it and force those memories in a nice little chest with a big lock. But when I lift the lid and examine the contents, there were some moments where simple human kindness kept me afloat for another week, or month. "Hey, you didn't answer my question. Are you gonna be all right?"

Beni's left hand reaches across and lands on top of mine. "Yeah. They said I was pretty dehydrated, something about my kidneys that they want to observe overnight, but they said I'll be free to go in the morning." He exhales. "I'll just take the bus back, Mitz. You don't need to buy me a ticket or anything. I never should've come up here. When someone disappears without a word, it's a pretty clear message." He swallows and looks away.

"Beni, I wanted to deliver the good news in person."

He turns toward me, and his brow wrinkles with concern. "Do I want to hear this?"

"Yeah, you do. The Duncan-Moon Philanthropic Foundation approved your application. They're going to fund your landscape design company."

Beni's features seem to freeze-frame. He sucks in a sharp breath, removes his hand from mine, and covers his eyes. Traitorous teardrops leak out from under his scarred hand. "I didn't even— I never filled out the—"

"You don't have to say anything. That's what friends do, Beni."

He wipes his eyes with the back of his hand and laughs. "You had me goin' there, Mitz. I thought you were gonna announce your engagement to Sheriff Perfect. Oh, man! You don't have to give me the money. I mean, let's call it a loan. I'll pay you back."

I lean back and slide my hand off his arm. "Listen, two things you need to get straight. One: it's Sheriff Too-Hot-To-Handle; and two: the only reason I'm funding your company is because I *don't* have to."

He opens his mouth to reply, but coughs instead.

I reach for the salmon-colored water pitcher and pour him a small glass.

He takes it gratefully, downs the water, and sighs. "For reals though, I can pay you back."

"You know what, Beni? I'd really rather you didn't. Just promise me you'll pay it forward someday. I'm starting to believe that's a better way to make the world go round."

His throat seems to have tightened up and he can't find words.

My extra senses pick up the waves of gratitude rolling off of him. "I'll be back in the morning after they release you. Silas will contact you with the details of the money you've been awarded from the foundation, and I'll drop you off at the airport. Do you need anything in the meantime?"

"Um, can you grab my bag from the motel?"

"Crapballs! We told her it was only for one

night. I better hustle over there and make sure she didn't send your belongings to the guild."

He laughs and drags a thumb under each eye. "What's the guild?"

"Oh, it's like the Salvation Army or the Goodwill. Don't worry. I'll get your stuff and settle your tab. You rest and get that business plan polished up."

He takes a deep breath, and I can almost feel the weight lifting from his shoulders. "I will. And I'm gonna ship you a cactus—special delivery. Although, the way you're turning into an ol' softy, Mitz, maybe I'll ship you a big basket of delicate, puffy hydrangeas instead."

I roll my eyes dramatically for his benefit, squeeze his shoulder, and head toward the door. Taking a pause, I glance back and say, "By the way, tomorrow, I'll be the one in the 1957 Mercedes 300SL silver gullwing coupe."

What slight color has returned to his face drains as he places one hand over his wide-open mouth and snaps the fingers of the other.

I wink and disappear.

CHAPTER 16

ERICK SENT A TEXT AN HOUR AGO, telling me it would only be thirty more minutes. He should know I'm not blessed with patience.

When the clock ticks thirty-five minutes, I fire off a text telling him I'm spoiling my appetite by eating some of Pyewacket's Fruity Puffs.

Turns out Pye's so happy to have me home in one piece that he doesn't even glare at me as I reach into the box of his sacred sugary children's cereal more than once.

At long last—

BING. BONG. BING.

Grams and I shouted in unison, "He's here!"

"Yes. And you are allowed a brief 'hello,' and then you are banished to the third floor of the printing museum until morning."

She crosses her arms and taps her perfectly manicured fingers. "Hm, joke's on you. You can't banish me when I've already decided I'll be working on my memoirs this evening."

"Are you still writing those? I thought you said you had a publisher interested."

"Well, you know how it is. I needed help to get the handwritten pages into a computer file. Stellen was so busy with finishing his last year of high school and checking out colleges . . . I wasn't quite finished writing anyway, so I figured I'd whip out another story or two and let him help me get it into some sort of electronic thingamajig next summer. There's no point in rushing." Her eyes sparkle with mischief, and I can't help but suspect she's keeping something from me.

"Yes, we all know what a full life you led."

She clutches her pearls and gasps. "Oh, you don't know the half of it."

A hesitant knock on the alley door reminds us both that we've ignored the doorbell.

Twisting the handle, I push open the door and wave him in. "Come in. Come in. Sorry! Grams and I were having a little debate. She's right there, and she would like you to know that she thanks you for saving me and will be retiring to the printing museum for the *entire* evening." The extra emphasis on the last sentence is entirely for Ghost-ma.

Erick lifts the unopened bottle of chianti and smiles. "Thanks for lifting the ban on wine. And I appreciate you giving Mitzy and I some privacy."

Fortunately, he can't hear her reply.

"You be sure to tell him that I never lifted any such ban, and I do not believe that alcohol is the solution to any problem."

I toss a fake smile her way and abuse my skills as an afterlife interpreter. "She says you're welcome and hopes we have a lovely night."

She surges toward me with an indignant swirl of ghostly energy. I chuckle while Erick shivers with a severe case of ghost chills.

However, she does keep her word and morphs through the wall into the museum after her tantrum.

Two orders of lasagna, half a basket of breadsticks, and an entire bottle of chianti later, I kick Pyewacket out of the apartment, and click off the lights.

So many people are fond of saying they slept like a baby, but from everything I know about babies, they don't sleep well at all. Crying, kicking, soaking through their diapers— I prefer to say I slept like the dead.

When I roll over and find the spot next to me

empty, I worry that I may have literally gone comatose.

As I'm about to fire off a text to my vanishing boyfriend, the bookcase door slides open and I yank the sheets up to cover my skimpy summer pajamas. He grins and flashes his eyebrows. "Good, you're awake. I ran over to Bless Choux and grabbed us a selection of pastries, including chocolate croissants, and two slices of bacon-and-onion quiche."

My eyes widen eagerly, and I lean forward.

"And two extra-large coffees." He raises the cardboard holder to show the proof.

"I knew there was a reason I loved you."

He sets the heavenly scented breakfast on the coffee table and scoops me out of the bed. "Are you saying you only love me for my ability to run errands?"

I drag my hand through his loose bangs and smirk. "No, I also love you for your ability to admit when I'm right."

He dumps me unceremoniously on the settee and shakes his head. "Always full of surprises, Moon."

Two bites of chocolate croissant down the hatch and a healthy glug of black gold, and I'm ready to face the bigger issues. "I have to take Beni to the airport this morning. What time are you planning to interrogate Deputy Candy?"

His shoulders slump. "You can drop the deputy part. The Birch County Sheriff's Department has officially rescinded his employment contract."

"Not much for rehabilitation then?" I wink teasingly.

"I think there are some very serious issues at play. I don't really feel comfortable joking about it. Plus, I could've lost you."

Shoving a large bite of quiche in my mouth, I avoid any comment. I've been wading through emotional muck for days. I can't take it anymore. "Fine. But no heavy conversations. I just want to enjoy my breakfast—"

Our eyes meet, our jaws drop, and we say it at the same time. "Silas!"

I lunge into my closet to put on absolutely anything, and Erick sends the text.

"Stand down, Moon. He said the diner is 'pandemonium,' and there's no place to 'seat oneself.' He's going to take his breakfast to-go, and he'll meet us at the pie-baking competition this afternoon."

I step out of the closet with my pants on, and, in my haste, a T-shirt that is one hundred percent inside out.

Erick chuckles, takes a seat on the sofa, and pats the spot next to him. "Let's relax and enjoy these last few minutes together before the weight of duty pulls me away from you."

"Deal."

Without bothering to fix my T-shirt, I flop down next to Mr. Wonderful and enjoy another croissant and the rest of my glorious java. "Did they find a body?"

Erick chokes on his cheese Danish and thumps his chest as he struggles to catch his breath. "I'm never going to get used to your left-field approach." He holds up one finger to keep me from launching any more queries while he takes a sip or two of coffee. "I assume you're asking about the dig at the Anderson farmhouse."

"You assume correctly. Although, I've always been told that when you assume it makes an—"

His blue eyes sparkle, and he shakes his head. "Don't go there. I have an update on the exhumation, but it didn't seem like breakfast conversation."

Wiping a little chocolate filling from the corner of my mouth, I lick it off my finger and lean toward him. "You've met me, right?"

He scoffs, and his warm smile touches my heart. "Oh, I've met you, Moon. But I'd be a fool to say that you don't continue to surprise me on a daily basis."

"I have to keep you guessing. That's what makes our relationship so dynamic, Sheriff Harper. Now what's the update?"

"Touché. They found a body, and—"

"And a vacuum!" Jolting upright, I blurt this out without thinking, completely stealing his thunder. "Please tell me she was buried with her vacuum."

Little lines appear between his eyebrows and he squeezes his eyelids down halfway. "How do you know these things? It's uncanny."

"It's not that uncanny. I saw her ghost, remember? She was pretty much vacuuming every time she appeared. And repeating this ridiculous mantra about how a woman's work is never done."

Erick's breathing becomes shallow, and he slowly places his cup of coffee on the table. Strange energy crackles between us.

"What is it? What's wrong?"

"What did you say? That last part. Just the last part."

"A woman's work is never done. The last time I saw her she—"

"You know I believe you when you say you can see and communicate with ghosts, but when—" He swallows and shakes his head. "There was a journal. One of the deputies found a journal hidden under a loose floorboard."

Even though I absolutely know what he's going to say next, and my extrasensory perception is firing information at me faster than a knife thrower at a carnival, I bite the inside of my cheek and keep my mouth shut.

"That phrase was written over and over on the pages. The journal will go a long way to corroborating the alleged abuse, but if I understand correctly, it will also absolve her husband of any potential involvement in her death."

"How is that possible? He locked her in that house. He strangled her, and then, you know, buried her in the basement to hide the murder."

He rubs a thumb along his jaw and sucks air through his teeth. "Maybe the ghost was lying to you. The medical examiner still has some work to do, to confirm the identity and cause of death, but according to the very detailed journal entry on the day she died, Phyllis Anderson fully intended to commit suicide. Her husband's doctor had prescribed her Thorazine, and she had been hoarding her meds. According to the notes written in her own hand . . ."

My attention drifts, because I already know this part of the story. She put on her best dress and her fancy hat, and now this new part that she previously omitted, about how she took a handful of pills. I've known about four or five ghosts since I arrived in Pin Cherry, and they're not always completely honest. Sometimes they make things up to fill in the gaps between what they know and what they've forgotten, but sometimes they purposely mislead. However, I've never met one who could put a vision into my head. That was some significant skill. Phyllis showed me her false version of murder. If I truly want to help her cross over, it seems like—

"Mitzy?"

Erick is on one knee in front of me, waving his finger in front of my face, and Grams is right behind him.

"It's happening! He's going to propose!"

"Simmer down, Grams. You've totally misinterpreted things—as per usual."

His gaze flips over his shoulder and he gets to his feet. "She's here, isn't she?"

"She absolutely is here. Full of her misguided theories and unauthorized thought-droppings. Grams, this is a direct invasion of privacy."

"Oh, don't be like that, dear. I saw him leave earlier this morning and return with breakfast. So I knew all the hanky-panky was over. And you said I was only banished for the night. It's clearly morning. Not to mention, I heard you talking about a strange ghost vision. You can't blame me for being intrigued."

I repeat some of her rant for Erick's benefit, and then address her assumptions. "I think the new rules will be that you're banished until I seek you out and invite you back into the apartment. That way, I get to decide when my date is over, not you. But you're right about the weird ghost vision.

Phyllis showed me what happened, but it wasn't what actually happened."

Erick waves his hand in front of my face. "Can you bring me up to speed?"

"Sure. Sorry. When Phyllis was telling me about how her husband killed her, she showed me the image of him strangling her, and her hanging in the basement. I was letting Grams know that it's the first time a ghost has ever given me a false memory like that."

To his credit he doesn't point at me and yell "Freak!" Instead, he nods and shoves his hands deep into his pockets. "I find that when perpetrators truly believe what they're saying, they can paint a very detailed picture of false events. Some can even pass a lie detector if they're truly convinced, and, oftentimes, clinically psychotic."

"So maybe the mental illness comes from Phyllis. Most likely her husband was an abuser—that seems accurate—but perhaps he locked her in the house for her own protection. I mean, it's a misguided solution, but it seems to fit better with the evidence."

He nods. "Based on the journal, the burial site, the vacuum, and your ghost-versations, I'm willing to unofficially ID the victim as Phyllis Anderson."

Tapping my fingernail on my front tooth, I run

through the current situation. "Where does that leave us?"

Grams swirls through him to get to me, and tiny ghost-bumps pop up on his forearms. "Mitzy, you have to help that poor woman cross over. She's been trapped in a purgatory of her own making."

She's right. "Can you get me back into the house, Erick? I think I know what I need to do to help Phyllis. If I'm right, it shouldn't take long to convince her to pass through the veil. I can meet you back at the station to interrogate Candy by 11:00 or 11:30. Sound good?"

He shrugs his shoulders and chuckles. "Funny, I keep thinking I'm the sheriff and I'm the one running the investigation, but I may as well change the sign on the front of the station to Mitzy Moon's Detective Agency."

I step through Ghost-ma and wrap my arms around the tall, understanding lawman. "You are absolutely in charge of the investigation. For the record, I *asked* if you could get me back into the house. I didn't command. But I do want to make it clear that leaving an earthbound spirit on this plane to wreak havoc on whatever family moves into that farmhouse next isn't in the best interest of your Birch County Sheriff's Department."

He kisses the top of my head. "I know when I've been beat. Let me make a call to get you the okay to go out to the house, and I'll reschedule Candy's interrogation for later this morning. Are you sure you'll be okay returning to that place all alone?"

To tell the truth, I hadn't really thought about it until he said it out loud. "I think so. I'll have to put on my big girl pants and do what needs to be done. Phyllis needs to leave, and I'm the one who has to conduct the eviction. I want to say that I'd love to have you waiting outside for me, but I do understand there's a fine line between boyfriend duties and sheriff duties. Your sheriff duties come first."

He tips his head in that way that insinuates he's doffing a cap, and smiles. "Well thank you kindly, ma'am."

"All right, smart alec. Make the call. I'm gonna turn my shirt right-side out and head out to the farmhouse."

"10-4."

CHAPTER 17

IT PAINS ME to admit how right Erick can be. As I ease down the long dirt road toward the Anderson homestead, my stomach is flip-flopping with negative emotions.

Beni and I could've died here. The fact that we didn't is simply a trick of fate.

If I didn't see ghosts . . .

If I didn't know how to pick locks . . .

If Beni wasn't in fighting shape . . .

The list of variables goes on and on. The main thing that concerns me is the effect Phyllis may have had on Lane. Is he suffering from a genetic mental illness, or was her presence in this home what pushed him over the edge into kidnap-prepper land?

It's almost as though I can hear Erick's voice in

my ear: "You do your ghost thing, Moon, and let me take care of the human criminals." He's right. My mission is clear.

Parking the Mercedes, I frown when I see the thin layer of dust covering my silver beauty. I'm tempted to run her through a car wash before I pick up Beni. However, vanity will have to be pushed to the bottom of my list.

Lifting the yellow crime-scene tape, I duck under and enter the empty dwelling.

My plan is slapdash at best.

In the tiny hall closet, I find what I'm looking for.

Rolling the current vacuum out of its parking place, I unwind the cord and plug it in. Without a word, I begin my meticulous back-and-forth pattern on the rug in the living room.

Phyllis pops into the visible spectrum with an audible crackle. "What are you doing? You better beat feet, dolly. That's my job. But those flatfoots took my vacuum. What am I supposed to do?"

"Good morning, Phyllis. I'm afraid you weren't completely honest with me the other day."

Her innocent housewife eyes turn dark and stormy. "Are you accusing me of being a shuckster?"

Keep vacuuming and play it cool. "Not exactly. I'm pretty sure you want to believe what you told me, but there's a part of you—deep down—that knows the truth. I want you to tell me the truth, Phyllis."

"You're just like him! I told you what happened. Why don't you believe me?"

Continuing my careful back-and-forth motion on the carpet, I let her stew in her own juices.

"He kept me prisoner."

"What was the medication your doctor prescribed?"

The storm clouds in her eyes spark with electricity. "My doctor?"

"We found your journal, Phyllis. There are no more secrets between us. What was the medication your doctor prescribed?"

She charges at me angrily, and I lift my left hand. My antique mood ring has protected me in the past. I don't know how or why, but whether or not this supernatural malarkey makes sense—it works.

Her apparition dissipates, and I hear a whimpering in the ether.

Switching the vacuum off, I leave it in the middle of the floor. The cord hangs limply over an unfinished job.

Phyllis snaps back into being. "You can't leave it like that. You have to finish. Complete the pattern or he'll be furious."

"I'll keep vacuuming, as long as you keep answering my questions. Do we have a deal?"

She clutches her pearls in panic and nods. "Yes. Yes. Just keep vacuuming."

"Fair enough." I turn it back on and continue the pattern. "The medication?"

"Thorazine."

"And how many pills did you take on that Easter Sunday in 1959?"

"No. No. He strangled me."

"Actually, I believe he was attempting to get the pills out of your stomach. I think he was trying to make you throw up. How many pills, Phyllis?"

"Fifty-seven. One for every week he kept me locked up. I used to halve my pills on the weekend and save the extras. I didn't know how many it would take, but I wanted to be sure."

Halved pills, whole pills, times fifty-seven . . . I'm not about to run the math. But she's finally being more honest with me, and that's what matters. "Tell me the story of that Sunday. The true story."

Her image wavers like oil on water, but she rewrites her tale. "He took our son to church and locked me in, as usual. I fixed my hair, made up my face, and put on my Easter dress. It wasn't new. He never let me leave the house at that point. But the frock was clean and freshly pressed. Then I cleaned the whole house, not just vacuuming. I dusted, I mopped the kitchen, and I put a ham in the oven. Once I finished vacuuming the living room, I went upstairs and pinned on a fancy hat. I counted the pills twice, to be sure, and then I took them."

"All at once?"

She presses a hand to her throat. "No, I couldn't swallow so many. I had to take them in three hand-fuls. With a very large glass of water." She floats over to the window and gazes across the vast acreage behind the farmhouse. "I went down into the basement. I wanted him to experience at least a few moments of panic when he returned. Didn't want him to be able to find me right away. But I didn't mean for the boy to find me."

My stomach churns. "Your son found you? Oh, Phyllis."

She presses both of her dainty hands to her face and chokes back a sob. "It's my only regret."

"I understand." I wasn't sure if I really under-stood, but it seemed like the right thing to say. Having sunk into some pretty dark places in my life after my mom passed, I'd wished I could join her more than once, but the thought of how it would affect the person who found me somehow kept me from acting on the thoughts. Maybe there's never just one clear reason why people do or don't.

"You said you'd keep vacuuming." She's shaking with nerves.

"Sorry, I got distracted." Snapping out of my unpleasant reverie, I continue pushing and pulling the vacuum across the old mint-green carpet.

"What happened next, Phyllis?"

"My son screamed. My husband ran down the stairs and sent the boy away. Then he buried me in the basement, and laid that infernal vacuum next to me. I suppose he thought that's all I was good for."

"Didn't you say he'd been telling everyone that you belonged in an asylum? Maybe he was telling them you'd left town, to cover up for your absences. He couldn't very well come out and admit he'd locked you in the house the whole time and then found you dead. Could he?"

"Who knows? I'm not sure what he told the folks at church. They definitely thought I'd skedaddled ages ago. The only person who knew I was around was his doctor, the one who prescribed the Thorazine. After— After he buried me, he called the doctor and told him I'd run off to my mother's. The doctor had never met me, just prescribed the pills on my husband's word, so no one ever checked."

"I'm so sorry, Phyllis." What else can I say?

"He took my son and moved away. It wasn't until Lane and his family came here one summer

that I found out about the name change—from Anderson to Candy—and the fact that I have a sweet
great-grandson. I didn't mean to drive him crazy.
You have to believe me. I just wanted to talk to him.
Hear about his life."

I want to feel sympathy or empathy for her situation, but after being held prisoner by her *sweet*
grandson, I don't have either of those things at the
ready. Time to focus up on my original mission.
"Phyllis, I'm going to finish vacuuming, and I'm
going to wind up this cord. And then it's time for
you to leave. It's time for you to cross over."

Her dark stormy eyes return to the innocent,
translucent blue and she nods. "I don't know how."

"I'm no expert, but you have to let go. You have
to release your attachment to this world. There's
nothing here for you anymore. We'll give you a
proper burial at the cemetery and make sure any
living relatives are notified of the location of your
gravesite. The details of your death will only be
known to the medical examiner, unless you want
them released."

"What do you think?" She places a small fist on
her hip and tilts her head earnestly.

It's a strange question that I absolutely was not
ready to field. "Honestly, Phyllis, I feel like your
family should know. If they had known about the
history of mental illness, someone might've gotten

Lane the help he needed, before things turned so ugly. I think you owe it to your descendants to let them know the truth."

Her apparition flickers, and I sense her hold on this plane weakening as I reach the edge of the carpet.

"I don't know why, but I trust you, Mitzy. You've been very honest with me."

Turning off the vacuum, I unplug the cord and carefully wind it up in the old figure-eight pattern that is bent into the cord like a bad memory.

Her image thins to a mere suggestion of the ghost that has haunted this home for so long.

Once I finish, I'm surprised to see that she hasn't gone.

A thought pops into my head unbidden and my claircognizance informs me to remove the bag and empty it outside. "Release the dust" is the phrase that slowly runs on repeat inside my brain.

As I unwind the cord to gain access to the bag, Phyllis regains a hint of her corporeal form. "What are you doing?"

"Hey, I'm pretty new to this. Apparently I missed a step."

She floats near me in confusion, but when I unzip the back of the vacuum and reach in to grab the bag, she screeches with fright.

The sound nearly pops me out of my skin.

"Take it easy, Phyllis. This is part of the process. You have to cross over."

She blasts through the wall in an attempt to escape her fate. And I'm extremely concerned about what she might bring with her when she returns.

Holding the dusty bag in two hands, I run outside, stand upwind and shake it furiously.

An invisible barrier traps her angry ghost at the front door and she screams unladylike threats as her ghost flickers and disapparates. She's definitely been trapped here too long.

In the end, I know I've done the right thing, and with her last earthly words she seems to relent. "Thank you."

Collapsing cross-legged on the grass, all the emotions I've been controlling so carefully spill out. Salty tears are streaming down my face, making streaks in the coating of dust on my hands and arms.

I refuse to take that bag back into the house.

Next to an outbuilding with sagging doors, there's a large fifty-five-gallon drum.

Drawing a ragged breath, I march toward it and toss the bag inside.

Swept up in the resolution of the moment, I dart back into the house and grab the vacuum.

In the middle of the dirt drive, I smash the vacuum like Prince with someone else's guitar and upend it into the same barrel as the bag. No one needs to get their hands on this possibly possessed little home appliance.

Washing up in the kitchen sink, I say a final goodbye to this strange and dangerous farmhouse.

Time to pick up Beni and get his fit little behind on a plane before he gets either of us into any more trouble.

An amateur sleuth's work is never done!

CHAPTER 18

WHEN I STEP into room 214, Beni is sitting list-lessly on his bed, looking like an extra from *One Flew Over the Cuckoo's Nest.* The mood ring on my left hand tingles and I look down to see an image of handcuffs wavering in the swirling black mist. The haunted look in his eyes tells me more than I need to know.

As I walk toward him, his gaze slowly lifts from the ground and he searches my face for a kind of comfort I can't offer. If my psychic senses are firing on all cylinders, simple human compassion should do the trick. "Hey, I'm having some trouble pro-cessing it all too. Why don't you get dressed, and let me take you to the airport. Put all this behind you and lose yourself in getting your new company off to a roaring start."

He rubs a hand across his chapped lips and scrapes the left side of his mustache with his fingernails. "Yeah. Yeah, that's what I should do."

Despite his apparent agreement, he makes no effort to hop off the bed.

"Did they put your clothes in that closet? Do you want me to—?"

"No. Leave it." His voice has a sharp edge, which sounds like anger on the surface, but my gift allows me to identify the fear still lingering beneath.

"Look, I get it. I went all ballistic on a vacuum this morning. Smashed it and stuffed it into a fifty-five-gallon drum, and definitely would've lit it on fire if I'd been rocking some matches."

My foolish comment breaks the tension, and he gets to his feet. "For reals? You sophomore-stuffed a vacuum?"

His reference to the high-school prank of shoving the underclassmen in lockers or trash cans, brings back some unpleasant memories. "Yeah. I'm crazy like that." I pull the strap of his backpack off my shoulder and swing it toward him. "How 'bout you grab some clean clothes from this backpack, and I'll see about getting you a little something for the flight?"

Beni grabs the backpack and hugs it to his chest. "Sounds cool. Haven't been on a plane since my boxing days, you know?"

"I didn't, but I wouldn't want you going three rounds with any of the passengers. Get dressed, slugger. I'll be right back."

Stepping out of his room, I close the door behind me and head to the nurse's station. After I drop the sheriff's name and reference Beni's recent trauma, the nurse agrees to ask the doctor for a couple of Xanax for Beni's flight.

He's buttoning his short-sleeve shirt when I return, but he still has no shoes on his feet.

"How about I grab your kicks from the cupboard and we leave the rest of your captive couture in there for the janitor?"

He presses his lips together and nods.

I retrieve the shoes and sit quietly. I wish I could tell him about Phyllis Anderson and the part her otherworldly influence may have played on Lane Candy's psyche, but the fewer people who know my secret the better.

The nurse I spoke to knocks sharply on the door and enters with a forced smile. "Here are your discharge papers, Mr. Alvarez." She hands him several sheets, explains follow-up visits with primary care physicians, and a series of other things Beni doesn't have and won't do. At last, she hands him the amber, white-capped prescription bottle. "Take one, two hours before your flight. If you are still experiencing anxiety, take a second before you board. Safe travels, Mr. Alvarez."

He swallows and accepts the bottle.

She offers me a perfunctory nod and exits.

Beni looks at the label and nods his approval. "Nice job, Moon. I'll hook you up if you ever head back to the AZ."

"I don't know about that, Beni. I'm finally happy where I'm at. No more running, no more searching."

He shoulders his backpack, motions for me to follow, and heads for the door. "I hear that, Mitz. I hear that."

In the hospital parking lot, my sweet ride gets the reaction I'd hoped.

Beni nods and makes several guttural expressions of awe as he circles the coupe and whistles. "Oh! You fancy now, Mitz!"

Blushing, I tell him to stow it and saddle up.

When the gullwing door rises, he exclaims, "You've gotta be kidding me!"

On the short ride to the airport, he chatters non-stop about the after-market upgrades he'd put on "her" and how much he could've gotten for "her" back in the day.

It's safe to assume he's referring to his grand-theft-auto days!

We end up booking a private charter to Chicago

where he'll grab his connecting flight to Phoenix. Turns out there aren't a lot of flights out of the Pin Cherry Harbor Airport that don't involve crop dusting!

I offered to wait with him, but he pushes me out the door. "You've done too much already, Mitz. The only way I'm going to be able to repay you is by designing an awesome garden—pro bono—for that library you're rebuilding."

Gripping his boxer's hand in both of mine, I bounce on my tippy toes. "Such a great idea. I love it. We can make it a sculpture garden, and I can involve the art students at the local community college. You really are the best, Beni. Looks like you might be making another trip to Pin Cherry after all."

He leans forward, lightly kisses me on the cheek, and slowly pulls away. "I don't think so. I can send you the plans electronically. You and I are on separate tracks now. Friends for life, Mitz, but on separate tracks."

Beni pulls his hand out of mine, and I wave wistfully as he wanders back into the small airport.

I only have ten minutes until the interrogation!

To be honest, I'm probably only three minutes from the sheriff's station, but I have no problem justifying my excessive speed with a series of hollow arguments. Beni was right when he called this car a bada** machine.

The deputy I've nicknamed Furious Monkeys is deep into her game when I come through the front door of the station. "Hey, what level are you now, Baird?"

She smiles, but never looks up from her screen. "I hit 302 just before you walked in. They keep releasing expansion packs, and I gotta beat them all!"

I never really got into video games. Sure, I lived with a couple of foster families that had low-end systems, but the controllers were always for the "real kids."

She bites the edge of her lip for a minute. "Head straight back."

"Thanks." Erick's office stands empty, so he's either already in one of the interrogation rooms, or he's escorting the prisoner. I'm in no mood to see "Candy, Lane" up-close and personal, so I dart into the observation room for safety.

There, in Interrogation Room 2, sits my kidnapper. Alone.

Looks like I was wrong about Erick's whereabouts. Maybe he's letting Lane sweat it out a bit. The diabolical young man stares deeply into the two-way mirror. A less psychic person might fear that he was looking directly at her, but I sense the stench of narcissistic pride wafting through the glass. His outward expression is rehearsed to show remorse, but inside he's deeply proud of what he was able to get away with.

My initial instinct to avoid confrontation vanishes as a surge of righteous indignation bubbles up from my gut.

Forcefully stepping into the hallway, I run directly into Erick.

He stumbles backward, catches himself on the wall, and manages to grab my arm before I take an unladylike tumble. "Good, you're here."

I chuckle as I regain my balance. "You know how I love a good entrance."

He squeezes my hand tenderly. "I'm about to start. Did you still want to wait in observation?"

"Nope. I've changed my mind. Maybe I need to face him on my own terms. I don't want him to think for one minute that he's going to get away with this. His twisted little mind is probably already prepping his insanity defense. I want to make sure he understands I plan to help the prosecution destroy that theory."

Erick leans back and raises an eyebrow. "That almost sounded like a threat."

"I can play dirty if I have to. He's dangerous. Not just to me, to anyone or anything that he target locks onto—"

Erick pulls me close to his chest and leans toward my ear. "I get it. You're welcome to join us. Let me get the tape started and handle all the particulars. Feel free to come in at any point."

He probably meant the whisper to be comforting and private, but my skin tingles with the heat of his breath and my palms are sweaty. "Copy that."

Stepping back into the observation room, I flip the silver toggle, and Erick's confident voice comes over the speaker.

When I see the sheriff seated across from the man-child, there's a distinct shift in Candy's energy. The pride he felt when he sat alone in the room has vanished. He's awash with respect and fear. He eagerly admits to everything, as though Erick is about to compliment him for his brilliant strategy.

The sheriff's tone never increases, and he gives no indication of how close this case is to his heart. He asks a series of prepared questions, which painstakingly place the former deputy at each scene, necessary to prove the state's case.

Candy verifies every bit of incriminating evidence, and even volunteers pieces of information that I had only psychically deduced.

Erick pauses and scans his notes.

The eerie whisper that floats through the speaker makes my skin crawl.

Candy wrings his hands and the chain scrapes

on the table. "I could've made her love me." His gaze is desperate and dangerous.

The sheriff pushes his chair back, stands, and towers over the mentally unbalanced former deputy. "You've clearly confused love with possession. No woman, especially not one as brilliant as Mitzy Moon, can be forced to love. You may have a high IQ, Candy, but you don't know the first thing about love." He leans over, clicks off the recording device, and saunters confidently from the room.

My heart is overflowing with admiration for Erick, and my need for vengeance—or whatever it was—has dissipated. I'll save my performance for the witness stand.

Before leaving, I take one last look at my captor. He's dangerously misguided, but he's in more need of proper medical attention than punishment. I may have helped put him in custody, but I'll leave his future in the hands of the professionals.

An icy jolt from my mood rings snaps me back to the present.

A delicious slice of pie flickers in the swirling mists.

Now that's the kind of message I'm in the *mood* to receive!

It's time for me to head over to the baking competition and cheer my surrogate grandfather to another victory—I hope!

CHAPTER 19

THE BIRCH COUNTY FAIRGROUNDS is a sight to behold. My mother may have taken me to a county or state fair at some point before she passed, but it must not have left much of an impression. This entire vista seems brand new.

There are four large, barn-size buildings anchoring the event. A sign on the closest says "Agricultural Hall," and a huge banner announcing today's competition adorns the structure. At the end of the next two buildings they've cranked the massive doors open wide to reveal a series of crafts in the one closest to the Ag Hall, and row upon row of fresh produce lining the exterior walls of the third building. Down the center are displays for the prized vegetable competition mentioned on the sandwich board in front of that structure.

The final enormous building is some distance away from the other three, and a young boy is currently leading a massive hog inside.

I'm going to go out on a limb and assume that's the livestock building.

Beyond him lies the midway, and what is sure to be a plethora of deep-fried treats.

A gaggle of 4-H-ers approaches, each carrying a stack of flyers. A tiny blonde girl in miniature Wrangler jeans, boots, and a 4-H T-shirt smiles brightly as she pushes a flyer into my hand. "Good afternoon. Are you going to the pie competition?"

"I am." I take the flyer and pretend to study it carefully.

"Gosh, that's the best event of the day, but don't miss the midway. The tilt-a-whirl is my favorite." Her eyes sparkle, and her excitement is infectious.

"Good to know." I smile at the rest of her young crew and head toward the competition building.

After stepping through the small door, within the larger door, I have to blink several times to get my bearings. There are over two hundred folding chairs arranged, with a wide center aisle leading up to an arc of six long tables covered with pies.

Wow! I think they may have actually undersold this event. The emcee is explaining the rules of the competition, but my attention is fully focused on finding an empty seat.

As if by otherworldly assistance, the shining pate of my lawyer and alchemical mentor beckons me from the second row.

I should've known he'd arrive early enough to get the good seats. Lucky for me, he had the foresight to save me one.

Hunching low to avoid interfering with anyone's competition experience, I sidle up next to the empty chair and slip in.

Silas Willoughby harrumphs, smooths his bushy grey mustache with a thumb and forefinger and wags his jowls. "That's cutting it pretty fine."

Leaning into the aura of pipe smoke and denture cream that always surrounds him, I whisper, "I had no idea it was such a big deal. I thought there'd be like twenty people in a back room somewhere."

He turns as his jaw falls open in shock. "Twenty people? At the county fair?"

"Hey, how was I supposed to know there was a whole fair?"

He steeples his fingers, exhales, and mumbles, "How indeed?"

Oh, I get it. If I was more in tune with my psychic gifts, I would've been able to predict every detail of what I'm witnessing. Touché, old wizard. Touché.

The only thing that catches my interest is when

the emcee stops prattling on and hands the microphone to Erick.

"Ladies and gentlemen, please welcome this year's Birch County Fair Grand Marshall and head judge of the pie-baking competition, Sheriff Erick Harper!"

The crowd erupts with applause, and several women whistle and catcall.

Suddenly, I'm very glad this is a pie-baking competition and not a bachelor auction. Some people have no manners.

He takes the mic and introduces the other two judges. "Welcome, folks. Helping me with this monumental task, we are lucky to have the hard-working Pin Cherry Harbor Mayor and the world-renowned Michelin star chef and owner of Yves Bistro."

The subdued applause never reaches the heights of the crowd's welcome to Erick. My boyfriend is more popular than the snooty chef. Personal triumph smirk: check.

The judges approach the first pie on the far left, pick up their forks, and each of them selects a plate.

The emcee has retrieved a second microphone and makes an announcement to the crowd. "This banana cream pie comes to us from the far northern regions of Birch County, baked by our oldest competitor, Artheta Estabrooks, who turns one hundred and three tomorrow!"

The audience once again breaks into a smattering of applause as I lean toward Silas. "They announce the name of the person who baked the pie? Don't they know that might influence the judges?"

Silas scoffs and leans so close his bushy mustache tickles my ear with his reply. "It's not hard to assume you missed the careful delineation of rules shared at the outset. These judges are chosen because they are unimpeachable. They are to judge the pie based on taste and presentation alone. No other information shall influence them. This is Erick's third year judging, but his first as Grand Marshal."

Well, shut my mouth. I didn't realize I was in the presence of living saints. Unimpeachable! Despite Silas and his belief, I doubt that very seriously. If announcing the names is tradition, I'm not going to argue with their precious tradition. But if it walks like a duck and it quacks like a duck, it can influence a judge. I'm just saying!

The names and pies are all blending together, but once we reach the double-crust section, and I hear the pin cherry pies announced, I lean forward, eagerly awaiting Odell's.

In the back of my mind, I imagine a cheesy announcer giving us the pie competition in comic play-by-play. "This is the moment you've all been waiting for. You may have paid for the whole seat, but you'll only need the edge!"

Silas elbows me. "Hush."

Oops. I may have inadvertently said that last bit out loud.

Erick tilts his head and struggles to remain professional. He's clearly biting the inside of his cheek to suppress a chuckle.

Yep, I definitely said that last bit out loud.

The judges have a noticeably improved reaction when they sample Odell's legendary pie. I cross my fingers, just in case that will help.

The trio of evaluators moves to the next entry and pick up clean forks. They turn in unison to face the audience, while waiting for the announcement to end.

"This late entry to the double-crust category is a twist on traditional pin cherry pie and comes to us from Phyllis Anderson."

The judges lift their plates and sink their forks into the slices as I lunge forward. Swinging my arm like an out-of-control batter, I slap all their plates to the rough concrete floor with an earsplitting crash.

The raucous crowd falls utterly silent, and Erick attempts to mumble without moving his lips. "What the heck, Moon?"

I push past him and grab the pie plate with its

remaining three slices. "Did you hear the name? Phyllis Anderson! He poisoned this pie. I don't know how it got delivered, or entered, but this is his final masterstroke. We can't be sure whether he put this part in place before the kidnapping or after the escape, but there is no Phyllis Anderson. She died in 1959!"

Mumbles and murmurs spread through the crowd like a lion rustling in the tall grass of the Serengeti.

The shocked emcee makes no effort to calm the crowd. Her arm hangs limp at her side and the fact that she still has a hold of the microphone shocks me.

Erick scrunches up his face and rubs his sexy jaw, but before he can confirm or deny my suspicion, there's a rhythmic click-slide-scrape that draws everyone's attention.

In the middle of the center aisle, a hunched woman with an oxygen tube running to her nose leans heavily on a walker. She clicks it forward a step, slides her feet, and scrapes her trailing oxygen tank along.

Uh oh.

The skin on my cheeks heats up, and I want this moment to end as soon as possible. I grab the spare mic Erick placed on the first table of pies and shove it into his hand. "I'm going to have another birthday before she gets to the front of the Ag Hall. Go. Go!"

He walks toward the elderly woman and tentatively holds out the microphone. "Ma'am, did you have a question?"

Her voice rattles in her throat and it seems the use of the voice box produces more dust than sound. If not for the microphone, no one would hear a thing. "I have a question. Why did that hot-tempered albino knock my pie on the ground?"

Erick's eyes widen, and he looks at me with concern. "Your pie? What's your name, ma'am?"

She balances precariously with one hand and grips the microphone with the other.

"Phyllis Anderson. Jourdan is my maiden name. I baked that pie yesterday and my niece had to deliver it. I can't carry much when I gotta take all this gear with me wherever I go."

And I'd like to be abducted by aliens now. Right now.

Ever the charmer, Erick comes to my rescue again. "Phyllis Anderson, you have my sincerest apologies. Let me get you a seat in the front row. The judges will all get fresh forks and plates, and give your creation a fair tasting."

Before she returns her free hand to her walker, she smacks his backside. "Get after it, young man. The Lord only knows how much time I've got left."

The crowd erupts with thunderous laughter and applause.

Silas jerks his head to the left and his jowls waggle frightfully.

Taking the cue, I dart out through a side door where I lean against the weathered wooden siding on the Ag Hall and laugh until I cry. All right, maybe I'm still processing my trauma. If I'm going to lose my marbles every time I hear the name Phyllis Anderson, I might need to reconsider my mental state.

Roughly five minutes later, Silas joins me. "Anyone in your situation would've performed with the same earnest conviction. If those people knew the complete story, not a soul in that hall would question your decision. I believe our good sheriff has patched things up, but I'm afraid your antics may have cost Odell the title."

"What? Why? They tasted his pie. I could tell they loved it."

"Indeed, but after the ruckus, one can only assume that if Mrs. Anderson's pie is even half as good as Odell's, they'll offer her the double-crust award just to smooth things over."

Sinking into the tall grass beside the hall, which escaped the lawnmower's blades, I drop my head in my hands and sigh. "Maybe I should just never leave the bookshop."

A familiar gruff voice penetrates my pity party. "Get up. You know I'd rather be safe than sorry every time." Odell's lived-in skin wrinkles around his eyes as his broad smile both absolves and mocks me.

As I get to my feet, he offers me a quick one-arm hug. "I'd rather have a living sheriff than a blue ribbon any day. You did right by me, Mitzy."

"Thanks. I'm really sorry if I cost you the competition. I'm such a klutz."

His pale-blue eyes sparkle and he pulls out the hand he's had behind his back the entire time. "I'll take the grand prize, 'Best in Show,' of the whole pie competition over a blue ribbon in the double-crust category any time."

The shock on my face is exactly the reward he was waiting for.

His raspy chuckle echoes off the old boards as he and Silas enjoy a lengthy bout of joviality at my expense.

"I'll hit you back, Odell. I don't know how, but I'll think of something." An enormous sigh of relief escapes from my chest. "I'd complain about your hijinks, but this is actually the perfect ending to a nasty week."

"I bet I could improve on perfection."

I turn toward Erick, and he leans in with a slice of pin cherry pie and a grin.

Before I accept the offering, I have to ask, "Is this the grand-prize pie, or the possibly poisoned pie?"

They all share another laugh while I stuff my mouth with purple-ribbon grand-prize pin cherry pie.

With friends like these . . .

End of Book 15

A NOTE FROM TRIXIE

Mitzy and Erick make a great team—and another case solved! I'll keep writing them if you keep reading . . .

The best part of "living" in Pin Cherry Harbor continues to be feedback from my early readers. Thank you to my alpha readers/cheerleaders, Angel and Michael. HUGE thanks to my fantastic beta readers who continue to give me extremely useful and honest feedback: Veronica McIntyre and Nadine Peterse-Vrijhof. And big "small town" hugs to the world's best ARC Team – Trixie's Mystery ARC Detectives!

As always, this book would not be the same without the insightful edits of Philip Newey. Any errors are my own.

I'm especially grateful for the thoughtful

wording provided by Mesa Fama for the suicide hotline information at the front of the book. She regularly contributes to *Medium.com*.

FUN FACT: I briefly participated in the 4H program, as a child!

My favorite line from this case: "This has to be the strangest investigation I've ever been on." ~Erick

I'm currently writing book sixteen in the Mitzy Moon Mysteries series, and I think I may just live in Pin Cherry Harbor forever. Mitzy, Grams, and Pyewacket got into plenty of trouble in book one, *Fries and Alibis*. But I'd have to say that book three, *Wings and Broken Things*, is when most readers say the series becomes unputdownable.

I hope you'll continue to hang out with us.

Trixie Silvertale (August 2021)

CAROLS AND YULE PERILS

Mitzy Moon Mysteries 16

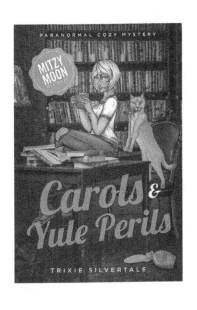

When a maple syrup mystery turns into murder, will this psychic sleuth's luck run dry?

Mitzy Moon can't wait to cut her own gorgeous Christmas tree. But her forest adventure loses its thrill when the pristine blanket of snow reveals a blood trail. And her heart thuds when the crimson droplets lead to a body, bringing her Yuletide festivities to a deadly end.

When her only employee becomes the prime suspect, Mitzy is forced to take the case. But even though she enrolls her eavesdropping Ghost-ma and a spoiled feline to help unwrap the evidence, each uncovered clue only seems to dig a more messy, murderous hole.

Can Mitzy unstick herself from the tacky case, or is her festive fun about to turn fatal?

Carols and Yule Perils is the sixteenth book in the hilarious paranormal cozy mystery series, Mitzy Moon Mysteries. If you like snarky heroines, supernatural intrigue, and a dash of romance, then you'll love Trixie Silvertale's twisty tinsel-clad tale.

Buy *Carols and Yule Perils* to wrap up the culprit today!

Grab yours here!
readerlinks.com/l/861835

Scan this QR Code with the camera on your phone. You'll be taken right to the Mitzy Moon Mysteries series page. You can easily grab any mysteries you've missed!

Once you're in the Club, you'll also be the first to receive updates from Pin Cherry Harbor and access to giveaways, new release announcements, behind-the-scenes secrets, and much more!

Scan this QR Code with the camera on your phone. You'll be taken right to the page to join the Club!

THANK YOU!

Trying out a new book is always a risk and I'm thankful that you rolled the dice with Mitzy Moon. If you loved the book, the sweetest thing you can do (*even sweeter than pin cherry pie à la mode*) is to leave a review so that other readers will take a chance on Mitzy and the gang.

Don't feel you have to write a book report. A brief comment like, "Can't wait to read the next book in this series!" will help potential readers make their choice.

★★★★★
Leave a quick review HERE
https://readerlinks.com/l/1834956
★★★★★

Thank you kindly, and I'll see you in Pin Cherry Harbor!

More to come!

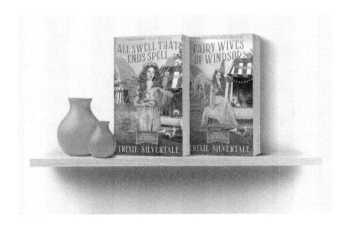

Explore the world of Coriander the Conjurer. A fortune-telling fairy with a heart of gold!

Book 1: ***All Swell That Ends Spell*** – A dubious festival. A fatal swim. Can this fortune-telling fairy herald the true killer?

Book 2: ***Fairy Wives of Windsor*** – A jolly Faire. A shocking murder. Can this furtive fairy outsmart the killer?

Join Sydney Coleman and her unruly ghosts, as they solve mysteries in a truly haunted mansion!

Book 1: ***Moonlight and Mischief*** – She's desperate for a fresh start, but is a mansion on sale too good to be true?

Book 2: ***Moonlight and Magic*** – A haunted Halloween tour seem like the perfect plan, until there's murder...

Book 3: ***Moonlight and Mayhem*** – An unwelcome visitor. A surprising past. Will her fire sale end in smoke?

ABOUT THE AUTHOR

USA TODAY Bestselling author Trixie Silvertale grew up reading an endless supply of Lilian Jackson Braun, Hardy Boys, and Nancy Drew novels. She loves the amateur sleuths in cozy mysteries and obsesses about all things paranormal. Those two passions unite in her Mitzy Moon Mysteries, and she's thrilled to write them and share them with you.

When she's not consumed by writing, she bakes to fuel her creative engine and pulls weeds in her herb garden to clear her head (*and sometimes she pulls out her hair, but mostly weeds*).

Greetings are welcome:
trixie@trixiesilvertale.com

BB bookbub.com/authors/trixie-silvertale

f facebook.com/TrixieSilvertale

O instagram.com/trixiesilvertale

Made in the USA
Las Vegas, NV
09 June 2024

90927502R00146